I0604012

CYNTHIA HICKEY

POISON BUBBLES

A Nosy Neighbor Mystery, Book 6

Cynthia Hickey

ISBN-13: 978-1-0879-8081-2

DEDICATION

To all my cozy reader fans who LOVE this series. Stay tuned, there's one more coming!.

ACKNOWLEDGMENTS

Thank you to God who keeps the ideas coming, and gives me the strength to work long hours, and to my husband and family who are willing to overlook a dirty house so I can write.

1

I hoped I would never have to shoot another person. "Why is my Glock in my suitcase?"

Mom peered through my open bedroom door. "Safety. You, Stormi Nelson, of all people, know you should never go anywhere without a gun or Tazor." She ducked back out.

I seriously doubted anyone at Mountain Springs Resort wanted to kill me. Still, Mom had a point. After our last horrifying ordeal of my niece, Cherokee, being abducted and almost sold as a sex slave, then being shot at and having to shoot someone, I knew things could escalate from good to bad in the blink of an eye. I sighed and slid my laptop in its padded bag. All I wanted to do from here on out was write my romantic mysteries.

"Oh, look!" My sister, Angela, entered the room and waved a pamphlet in my face. "Wear something nice. They have a semi-formal party every Saturday night."

I shook my head and rolled my little black dress into a corner of the suitcase. My sister thought of herself as a fashion icon, but really, I'd place her more in the "lady of the evening" category. Still, the resort trip was, hopefully, a healing time for us. I bit my tongue and continued packing.

"Hey, beautiful." My fiancé, Matt, stepped behind me and wrapped his arms around my waist before nuzzling my neck. "I'm going to miss you."

I turned and slipped my arms around his neck. "Come with us."

"I can't. I'm leaving for an undercover job in Little Rock."

"Then, you'll only be half an hour from us. Try to visit.

He chuckled. "I'll try, but two weeks at a swanky resort isn't exactly a hardship for you."

I gave what I hoped was a sexy pout. "It will be without you."

He planted a quick kiss on my lips. "I'll call as often as I can." He tapped my nose. "Try and stay out of trouble."

"No promises." Seriously, how much trouble could I get into at a resort where every hour contained a planned activity? I probably wouldn't write a single word.

He kissed me again. "Relax and have fun." With a wink, he strolled out the door.

A quick glance at the clock warned our departure time was approaching. Who was I kidding? I'd never left the house once on time since my family moved in. We'd be at least a half hour late.

We were an hour late. I leaned against the van I'd rented, not trusting Mom's old thing to get us anywhere safely, and stared across the street to where Rusty tried to mow his yard on crutches. After taking a bullet for my mother, the simple man would always hold a special place in my heart. Still, enough time had passed, he shouldn't need the crutches.

"You can put your crutches in the closet now, Rusty."

He nodded and rushed into the house.

"I still don't know why I can't go with you." My nephew, Dakota, wheeled his mother's suitcase to me. "Wayne works all the time. I'll be alone and bored."

"He said he would take off part of the time and you two would have loads of fun." Other than Matt, Detective Wayne Jones was the next best person to watch over my sweet nephew.

"Thank you for inviting me," Maryann, my best friend, literary assistant, and soon to be sister-in-law, dragged a suitcase behind her. "This is going to be fun."

"You deserve it as much as the rest of us." After all, when Matt's cover was blown and he was scheduled for execution by his abductors, it ripped her apart as much as it did me. This mini-vacation was desperately needed by all of us.

I reached through the van window and pressed the horn. "For crying out loud, we'll be driving in the dark!"

Suitcases started flying out the front door. My nephew rushed to gather them and shove them into the back of the van.

"We're running out of room," he said, pushing his back against one.

"Tell me those aren't mostly your mother's." I glared at my sister taking mincing steps in way too high of heels toward us.

"They are," he said.

"Take the two smallest ones out. She can carry them in her lap." I crossed my arms. "It's two weeks, Angela. They have free laundry. You need ten outfits, max."

"And accessories, shoes, makeup," she counted off on her fingers. "Not everyone is happy going all natural like you."

"I'll take that as a compliment." I closed the back of the van as the others piled inside, then slid behind the steering wheel. We waved and blew kisses at Dakota as we backed out of the drive.

He stomped away, not returning our gestures. Poor boy. He'd been as worried as the rest of us when everything turned bad a month ago. But, I had been outvoted in letting him come along.

An hour later, we pulled into the resort as the sun kissed the top of the Ozark mountains. We were met by two very handsome young men who set to work loading the mound of luggage onto a wheeled cart. A blond woman in a suit and sensible heels waited on the veranda.

She smiled. "Welcome to Mountain Springs where you're treated like royalty. My name is Cheri Mason. Please, allow me to show you to your rooms."

I was bushed and my nerves stretched to the breaking point by the drive. Non-stop chatter was never my thing.

She led us to a cottage at the rear of the resort. "There are two bedrooms, each containing two queen-size beds. We've spared no expense to give you a luxurious experience during your stay here. In both bathrooms, you'll enjoy a rain style shower head and a tub big enough for two. There is an assortment of lotions and bubble baths for your pleasure. We have free Wifi and a five star restaurant. Enjoy." She flung open the French doors and stepped back.

"I get the bath first," I raced in and stopped, staring around me in awe. Everything was white except the dark wood floor, polished to a high sheen. Sheer curtains fluttered at the open window. The chilly breeze let us know we had entered autumn.

"There is champagne, non-alcoholic cider, fruits and cheeses in the fridge," our chirpy hostess said. "If you need anything else, give us a call. Someone will be right over." She closed the doors and left us alone.

"Wow." I was bound to spill something on something. White was not my friend. It was beautiful, though. I could already feel the tension easing from my neck and shoulders.

I wheeled my one large suitcase into the room I would share with Maryann and left it next to one of the beds. Ten minutes later, a glass of sparkling cider in one hand and a scented candle in the other, I stepped into the bathroom, smiling with glee at the sight of the massive claw footed tub.

I ran the water, poured in something smelling of flowers and musk, then lowered myself into water barely out of the range of too hot. "Ah." I sighed, settled back, and closed my eyes.

When the water cooled, I added more hot. This was the life. Maybe, I'd make it an annual pilgrimage.

"How much longer!" Angela pounded on the door.

"Use your own."

"Mom has been in there forever."

"Not my problem. Go away. I'm relaxing." I closed my eyes and sank under the bubbles. Unfortunately, I could still hear her, although she sounded like a fish garbling.

She pounded some more, then silence. I popped over the bubbles and opened my eyes, then raised the rest of the way. The water was cooling quickly from the open window. I lifted my hand and studied my prune-like fingers. It was time to let Maryann in.

I stepped out onto a plush white towel and reached for my robe.

A scream shattered the peaceful night, ripping through my window like an icy claw.

I shoved my arms into the armholes and tied the sash in a knot around my waist as I burst from the restroom, through the bedroom, and into the living room. "What was that?"

The other three stood in a tight circle like warriors, backs together, watching for danger.

"It sounded like a woman."

"Someone is being killed."

"Tortured!"

Everyone spoke at once, except for my niece. Her dark eyes were wide, her skin pale as she stared at the front door.

A knock at the door had us all spinning and shrieking like girls at a slumber party after watching slash and gore movies.

I waved them to be quiet and retrieved my gun from my suitcase before slowly opening the door.

Cheri stood, the ever-present smile in place. "Just a cougar, ladies. Nothing to be scared about. You'll hear them every night, most likely. My apologies for not telling you earlier. Have a good evening."

At least I'd had my bath before the craziness started. "I'm going to put on my pajamas. Maryann, the tub is all yours." Dropping my Glock back into my purse, I headed for the bedroom.

I donned a pair of red and white polka-dot cotton shorts and a red tank top, then dug in my suitcase for the latest mystery I'd purchased. I wrote them, and read them, with a voracious appetite.

"Don't you get enough of murder and death?" Angela lay sprawled across an easy chair and filed her nails. "Read something sexy. Oh, wait…that word isn't in your vocabulary."

I decided not to comment. Matt didn't seem to have a problem with me and his was the only opinion that mattered. I rolled my eyes and took up half the sofa. "I'm here to relax and enjoy myself. Where's Cherokee?"

"I let her take my turn in the tub."

"That was nice of you."

"She was shook up after the cougar scream."

That had definitely gotten the blood flowing. I opened the book and started to read, getting engrossed in a murder mystery that had nothing to do with me. How sweet it was.

Soon, all five of us were sitting quietly, involved in our own methods of relaxation. Tomorrow, we'd have massages and three course meals. Maybe a walk through the garden after breakfast. Pretty much whatever we wanted. The resort offered everything from yoga to makeovers, including a designer dress shop. Maybe I would update my wardrobe. I smiled, knowing I didn't have to do anything but veg out if that was what appealed to me.

I glanced at Cherokee, relieved to see the color had returned to her face. After her kidnapping, she'd cut her waist length mane of raven black hair to shoulder length. If her plan was to look less pretty, it didn't work. Instead, the shorter cut emphasized her high cheekbones, courtesy of her Indian father who decided life on the reservation was better than raising a child. I vowed right then and there to make sure my niece returned home with no more ill effects of her ordeal. At least what was in my power to remove.

I turned my attention back to the story printed on paper.

"Help!"

I bolted to my feet and yanked open the front door.

"Gun!" Mom shoved my purse in my hands.

A woman, clad in a flimsy white nightgown, raced toward the main building. "He's dead! Oh, my, god, he's dead."

2

With my purse slung over my shoulder, I followed the fleeing woman. By the sound of pounding feet behind me, I guessed the other four followed.

We barged into the common room at the same time as the distraught woman. I turned her to face me. "What happened?"

"My husband. He's dead. In the tub." She keeled over like a weak tree in a tsunami.

While the others helped her to a sofa, I greeted an unsmiling Cheri, who looked as if she'd been in the process of getting undressed. She wore a robe over the skirt to her suit. "Please do not tell me that you are the type of guests to cause problems," she said.

"Quite the contrary. Which cottage is this woman in?"

She peered around me. "Twelve." She jangled a set of keys. "Would you accompany me, please. I see you're well armed." She motioned toward the butt of my gun sticking from my purse. "Just in case of trouble, you know."

"Call an ambulance," I told Mom, then followed Cheri across the thick grass to cottage twelve. Her keys weren't needed. The door stood open in invitation.

We exchanged a tense glance, then cautiously stepped inside. "Mr. Granger?" Cheri's voice sounded abnormally loud.

"You check the bedroom," I said. "I'll check the bathroom."

I regretted my choice the moment I set foot in the white-tiled room. A man, I presumed to be Mr. Granger, lay in a tub of fading bubbles. He might have been handsome in life, but now his mouth hung open in agony as he had drawn his last breath. "I found him. How long until the authorities get here?"

"Oh, my. They're on their honeymoon. How sad." Cheri stopped in the doorway and clapped a hand over her mouth. She mumbled something, then removed her hand and repeated, "Twenty minutes. The resort is in the country for a reason. No one can relax with the sounds of sirens."

Just cougars and screaming women. "We'll have to keep others from entering. Go meet the ambulance, and I'll sit outside the door."

She nodded and hurried away.

I studied the corpse, not finding any reason for his death. Had the poor man had heart problems? He looked to be in his late twenties, but it wasn't unheard of. I squatted and peered under the tub. Nada. One of the man's hands was in the water, the other hanging limp over the side. I averted my gaze from water now devoid of bubbles. In the hand I could see clearly was what looked like a worm. I peered closer. What in the heck was it?

Maybe an inch long and gray in appearance it seemed to be the leg of an octopus. I shuddered. I'd tried pickled octopus once and couldn't stand the taste or the texture. Maybe it was meant to be an aphrodisiac of some sort.

I left the bathroom and dragged a kitchen chair outside with me. The night carried a definite chill, that, combined with the vision I'd left in the cottage, left me shivering and wishing I'd worn my robe outside.

After what seemed a very long time, sirens wailed in the

distance, joined shortly by a coyote's howl. What other creatures did these woods hide?

Mom arrived and draped a blanket around my shoulders. I snuggled into the warmth and told her what I'd found.

"The poor man." She scooted against me until we were both sitting one-cheeked on the chair. "His wife is devastated."

"Can you buy pickled octopus in Northern Arkansas?"

She wrinkled her brow. "I'm sure you can at specialty stores. Don't go looking for trouble, Stormi. I'm sure we'll find out he died of natural causes."

I shrugged. "I hope so." Still, I'd learn to trust the niggling sensation at the base of my skull and it was shouting foul play, although I had absolutely no facts to base the feeling on.

Cheri led two police officers and two paramedics to the cottage, then stood next to me while they entered. "This is horrible."

"Who found the body?" The burliest man I'd ever seen glared down at us.

I raised my hand. "I'm Stormi Nelson, author and private investigator."

"Drumming up business, Miss Nelson?"

I made a noise in my throat. "No. I'm on vacation."

"You're the one who brought down the trafficking ring a few weeks back."

"Yes." I stood, keeping the blanket tight around me. "We heard Mrs. Granger screaming that her husband was dead, then Cheri and I came to check on him. He was dead when I found him."

His pen scratched across a small pad he held. "How do you know? Did you check?"

"Look, officer…" I squinted to make out the name on his badge, "Rodriquez. When someone's chest isn't moving and their lips are blue, it's a pretty good indication they're dead."

"Hmm." He wrote something else, keeping the pad angled so I couldn't see. "Just so long as you don't decide to interfere in our investigation during your vacation. Stick around for a while, in case we have more questions."

"We're here for two weeks." Two weeks that now promised to be long ones. "Are you suspecting foul play?"

"Just routine." He gave a thin-lipped smile and joined the other officer inside.

"He isn't telling us something." Mom craned her neck to follow him.

"I didn't see anything suspicious. I think he's unpleasant in nature."

"A murder will not look good for the resort." Cheri paced the brick walk. "Not at all."

"A man died," I said, glaring. "There's more at stake than bad publicity."

She waved a hand, dismissing my words. "I know. I'm sorry, but these types of things don't happen around here. I have no precedence for handling this type of situation." She glanced toward the thick trees as another coyote howled. "That's the type of injuries we have, rarely, but there has been a wild animal attack or two when hikers are careless."

By midnight, we were informed we were free to return to our own cottage. I collapsed in bed and pulled up the thick quilt to rid myself of the last traces of a chill, and said a prayer for the poor widow left behind.

Pounding on the door woke me the next morning. I groaned and rolled over. Did no one on the resort sleep in? When the knocking continued, I tossed the blankets aside and shuffled to the front door.

Mrs. Granger stood on the bricked stoop. "I heard you were a PI?"

"Yes?" I'd recently obtained my license in order to snoop

legally.

"I want to hire you to find my husband's killer?"

I blinked away the sleep. "Excuse me? Did the authorities determine it wasn't a natural death?"

"They haven't said. May I come in?"

By now, my family was gathering. I let Mrs. Granger inside and motioned for her to sit at the table.

"I'll make coffee," Mom said.

There were only four chairs so the rest perched wherever they could and stared at the widow. She paled under the scrutiny and cleared her throat several times until Maryann brought her a glass of water. "Thank you. My name is Amber Granger. My husband, Seth, was in perfect health. I know this because," she took a deep breath, "I made him get a full medical work up after I caught him cheating on me a few months before our wedding. All the tests came back fine. I think his cheating girlfriend killed him."

I glanced at Maryann, then back to Amber. "Who is she?"

"I have no idea." Amber set her glass down with a thump. "This was our second honeymoon in six months in a vain attempt to save our marriage." She blinked rapidly. "I loved him dearly, but he was a cheating bastard."

We had our number one suspect, if, in fact, Seth had been murdered.

She met my gaze. "Will you take the case? Money is not a problem. Seth left me very well off."

The hole kept getting deeper, except experience had taught me it wasn't usually the most likely suspect. "Sure, why not?" There went my vacation. I could have refused her request, but it might make a good novel, and I did want references for my investigating. "Where can we reach you?"

"Here." She sighed. "We paid for a month. They put me in a suite in the main house. I couldn't stay in that cottage a moment longer." She declined coffee and let herself out.

"I thought we were here to have fun." Cherokee rolled off the back of the sofa and onto the seat with all the dramatics of a wronged teenage girl.

"We can do all the things we planned," Angela said, tossing me a dirty look. "Let them work."

Suited me fine. My sister tended to go off half-cocked when 'trying to help'.

Mom poured coffee and handed us all mugs. "What first?"

"I figure if the girlfriend did kill Seth, then she must be a guest here. We somehow get a copy of the guest list and start interviewing." I blew on my drink before taking a sip. I grimaced, missing the frozen coffee my friend Norma made.

"I'm going through with my massage," Mom said. "Those gals like to talk. If there's any gossip to be had, they'll know it."

"Great idea!" I'd keep my appointment, too. The vacation didn't need to be a total waste.

I glanced at my watch. "Breakfast is in fifteen minutes."

We all stampeded to our rooms. Since meals were included in the price, I, for one, did not intend to miss a single one. I struggled into a pair of skinny jeans and a long-sleeved blue tee shirt, slipped my feet into flats, and met Mom on the way out the door. If the others missed the buffet, which ran for one hour, that was their problem.

I slipped my arm through hers. "I love you."

"Ditto, child." We practically skipped to the restaurant, excited beyond belief to eat a meal we didn't cook. I had a freezer at home full of casseroles I'd baked while under stress, and Mom ran the bakery we were partners in.

By the time we sat at a table, the others trickled in and joined us. I almost didn't recognize my sister without her makeup.

"Don't look at me. I'm hideous," she said. "But I have a facial right before my massage. Why put on makeup?"

In my opinion, she wore too much anyway. She was pretty enough without any.

I dug into my omelet and studied the other guests lining up at the buffet. Most looked to be couples on their honeymoons or on getaways. Maybe Amber was wrong about her husband's death. Unless one of these people were cheating with Seth against their spouse, I would have to look in a different direction.

"We need a way of getting the guest list." I set my fork and napkin on my plate. "It's most likely on a computer."

"A diversion?" Mom tilted her head. "Something that lasts long enough so you can go into the office?"

"Yeah." I took my lip between my teeth.

"Leave it to me." Mom stood.

Oh, no. The last time she created a diversion we'd almost been killed.

I frowned as she headed outside, then burst back through the doors.

"A cougar! Right out there. It's stalking a child. Oh, somebody help."

I almost lost my breakfast. But, it worked. Everyone in the restaurant, left like a giant wave. I went to the annex, pleased to see that the young man behind the counter was also gone. Hopefully, Mom's ploy would work long enough for me to print off a list.

There were twenty-four cottages, all rented. I printed off the sheet I needed and rushed back to the customer side of the counter and went to join the milling crowd.

When Mom saw me, she shrugged, "I'm sorry. I must have been mistaken. It was only a cat." She pointed to an orange tabby and grabbed my arm, pulling me toward our cottage. "Did you get it?"

"Yes. Try to be a little more believable with your diversions. They get crazier with each passing day."

"But," she pointed at the sky, "they work! Now, let's go find a killer."

3

I loved my mother's enthusiasm, most times, but her zeal was a bit much before noon. We spread out the two pages I'd printed in the resort office on the kitchen table and stared at them as if a name would magically shout, "I did it!"

"It's time for our massage. Maybe something will come to us while a stranger gets too personal."

Mom laugh. "Pray we get Chatty Cathy."

"Who?"

"Never mind." She sighed as if I was the densest person on the planet and headed out the door.

I scooped up the list and followed. "Who is Cathy?"

"It's a doll. You pull her string, and she talks as often as you want her to. Before your time, I guess."

Mom had dropped hints of feeling old ever since her serious boyfriend turned out to be the ring leader of the trafficking ring I had a hand in bringing down. At fifty one, she was still gorgeous with her trim figure and red hair. Someday, she'd find a man worthy of her. Someone like Dad, maybe, if God made more than one of the best men ever created.

I missed him every day. His unsolved murder played a big part in my playing the sleuth on a regular basis. I *needed* to see justice served.

I opened the door to a gazebo styled building and let

Mom enter first. A girl with a too-big smile and a bouncy ponytail greeted us from behind a bamboo counter. "Welcome. I'm Amy. You must be Mrs. and Miss Nelson. Please, follow me."

If everyone at Mountain Springs took happy pills, I was in the wrong place. I exhaled sharply and followed her to a room filled with sunshine and two massage tables. Two more overly-happy girls waited.

"This is Bri and Lisa. They'll be taking care of you," Amy said, closing the door behind her as she left.

"I'll take you," Bri said, motioning to one of the tables. "I'm a huge fan."

Great. Maybe I could get her to spill the gossip on the other guests. I lay on my stomach and rested my face in the hole designed for that purpose.

Bri giggled. "I need you to strip down, first. You may leave your panties on."

Oh. I glanced around for a place for a modest person to strip. In the corner, a three-paneled partition welcomed me. A few minutes later, wrapped in a thick towel, I resumed my place on the table. Mom, dropped her clothes where she stood and climbed onto her own table.

"Are you working on a new book?" Bri asked, kneading my shoulders.

"I'm mulling something over." I groaned and closed my eyes as her fingers dug deeper.

"Have you thought of writing about a murder at a spa and resort? There are all kinds of quirky people staying here." She moved her hands down my back. "With the death of Mr. Granger, you have a start. I'd love to be a character in one of your books."

"Remember that quick trip you took to Vegas, Stormi?" Mom asked. "We don't want a repeat of that. Or that time the crazed fan wanted you to hurry and write."

Exactly. A woman, wanting to be involved in a mystery before dying of cancer, and killed someone in order to help me solve the crime. Bri's remark was dangerously close to that very concept. Could it be possible to have the same motive here?

"I'm not thinking of books, really," I said. "It doesn't mix well with vacation."

"Oh, pooh." Bri started pounding with small, quick motions. "The things Lisa and I could tell you."

"We aren't supposed to gossip with the guests," Lisa said.

"That's all right." The vinyl under Mom whispered as she moved. "We're good at keeping secrets. Entertain us. You don't have to use last names."

I grinned. Mom was excellent at getting to the point.

"Well," Bri began, "there are rumors that Mrs. Granger is now the recipient of a large insurance policy. Oops. I used her last name. Oh, well. That isn't a secret." Her hands stilled. "The head waiter is making eyes at Cheri, but he's a few years too young, I'd say. The older couple, Bill and Ida are the cutest thing, all gushy gushy around people, but I've seen them when no one was looking and they hate each other!"

So far, none of them seemed to have a motive to kill Seth.

"Mr. Granger was very good looking," Lisa said. "Maybe he was fooling around with one of the gals in that bridal party."

"Good one, Lisa!" Bri resumed the massage, digging a little too hard for comfort. Was she using her elbow? "That's right. We have a party of eight, counting the future bride, staying in cottage thirteen. The girl's last hurrah before tying the knot. Oh, I know! He was making eyes at one of them, and his wife offed him."

We were getting nowhere fast. "Are all the names listed on the guest list?"

"No, just the one who booked the room. Although, Cheri keeps a log somewhere for emergencies. How would you know that?"

"Uh, a guess. That's a strange way of keeping records."

Bri leaned close to my ear. "Some people who come here don't want it known that they are here. Capice?"

I got it all right. The beautiful Mountain Springs was not all that it seemed. "Tell us some funny stories."

"Well—"

"Good morning, ladies." Cheri's voice drifted through the room like an unwelcome mud slide. "I trust you are getting relaxed and ready for your facials. They start in fifteen minutes. I'm afraid I need to hurry your massage along as there are other guests waiting, and you've gone over your allotted hour." A door closed.

"That woman is a burr in my bobby sock." Bri pulled the towel from my waist to my shoulders.

I'd be scheduling another massage with the talkative Bri as soon as possible. "Do you give private massage sessions? I'll pay you."

"We aren't supposed to. That would be grounds for dismissal."

Keeping the towel around me, I sat up. "Too bad. I'd like to hear more about these lively characters. I'm afraid nosiness is one of my traits." I smiled up at her. "If I use any of the information, changing the names, of course, I could name you in the acknowledgments of the book."

She glanced at Lisa, who shrugged. "I have an opening day after tomorrow at nine a.m."

It was better than nothing. I slid off the table and headed to the modesty panel to get dressed. My legs barely held me up. All tension was gone. Bri had done a wonderful job.

Angela burst into the room. "Way to hold things up."

And, the tension was back. I sighed, mumbled an apology, and squeezed past her to head to my facial.

The next woman didn't fit any of my preconceived ideas of what you needed to look or act like in order to work at the resort. Alice, according to her name tag, resembled a bull dog in shoulder width and facial expression.

I reclined in a padded chair mere seconds before a hot rag was dropped onto my face. "Ow!"

"Leave. It good for pores." Her thick German accent garbled over me. "Don't be baby."

I doubted I would get any news out of her. Instead, I closed my eyes and let myself be tortured by waxing, tweezing, and some stringent liquid that stung my newly opened pores. What a woman does for beauty. When my torturer smeared a silky lotion over my face, I sighed in relief at the coolness.

"Rest. I back in twenty minutes. Do not move face." Heavy footsteps padded across the floor, then a door closed.

"Stormi?" Mom whispered.

"I didn't know you were in here."

"Yeah, I must have had your gal's sister. These two aren't much for talking. I was afraid to ask any questions."

"Stop talking. Face will crack." I think it was Alice who moved my chair to a sitting position. She gently wiped my face with a lavender scented cloth. "Me and Ada are nice girls. What you want to know?"

"You wouldn't happen to know whether Mr. Granger was murdered, would you?"

She laughed, the sound soft in comparison to her speech. "No, only the po-lice will know that. You a funny girl."

"Can you tell me whether the resort sells octopus?"

"The kind in a jar or the kind in a tank?"

"Either."

"Yes, in a jar. Very good." She stepped back and studied my face. "You very pretty. No go sticking nose in places it not belong and ruin my work. Nose might get cut off. Now go. Next guest is here."

I skedaddled as if she chased me out with a paddle. After the massage and a facial that left my face as smooth as a newborn baby's bottom, I didn't want to do anything but take a nap. Further investigation into Seth's death would have to wait.

I woke to the sound of my cell phone ringing. I reached for it and knocked it to the floor. After several seconds of leaning over the bed fishing for the phone, I picked it up and noted Matt's number. "Hey!"

"Hello, gorgeous. How are you?" He sounded sleepy.

"Relaxed and taking a nap. How's the undercover work?"

"Well...I was shot last night."

"What?!" I bolted out of bed. "I'm coming to you. Where are you?"

"Stay relaxed," he chuckled. "Wayne, myself, and your nephew, just rented a cottage vacated that morning. I have strict orders to take some time off. Would you answer your door, please?"

My door? I padded in my bare feet to the front door and yanked it open. There stood the man of my dreams, his arm in a sling, and wearing a crooked smile.

I burst into tears and threw my arms around his neck.

He grunted and staggered back. "Careful. I'm wounded."

"I'm sorry." I gave him a lingering kiss and dragged him inside by his good arm. Wayne and Dakota followed. "Does Maryann know you're here?"

"No. She won't be happy when she finds out why. My little sister worries more than you."

"I got to come after all," my nephew said with a grin. "Where's my mom?"

"Beautifying." I led Matt to the sofa. "What can I do for you?"

"Give me another kiss." The corner of his lips twitched. "It's the best medicine in the world."

I fulfilled his request, then sat on the coffee table and looked into his eyes. "I'm working."

"Define working." He frowned.

I told him about Seth's death, the octopus tentacle, and the grieving widow hiring me. Then, I regaled him with all I had learned during my facial and massage. "But, now that you're here and needing my nursing skills—"

He laughed. "Spare me that, please. Keep the assignment. I'm not a good patient, and this will help take my mind off the fact I'm benched for a few weeks. I'm also privy to information you can't get access to. Do you think we can get into the cottage where the death occurred?"

"What number are you in?"

"Twelve."

"You're already there."

4

Matt opened my laptop and tapped the keys with one finger. "I'm looking for the police report and the autopsy. If we know exactly how Seth Granger died, we'll know where to start looking. It's possible he died of natural causes despite what his wife says. If he did, there is no case."

I sat in anticipation while he stared at the screen, typed, and stared at the screen some more. When I couldn't hold in my nervousness, I paced. The whole waiting thing was putting a damper on any good the massage had done. "Nothing? It's been fifteen minutes."

"Hold on." Wayne laughed, shaking his head. "These things take time."

"Got it." Matt straightened. "He was definitely murdered. His body contained a toxin only found in a tiny jellyfish, called Irukandji, native to Australia. So...how did these little killers get into Granger's bubble bath?"

"Wouldn't someone have found them?" My heart stuttered. I was never getting into water that wasn't crystal clear. "Wouldn't someone else have been stung when they pulled him out of the tub?"

"Not if they were wearing gloves." Matt closed the laptop. "They're as small as my fingernail and probably went down the drain when the plug was let out. I doubt anyone looking would have noticed anything. They probably looked like the bubbles."

"Grown men shouldn't take bubble baths," Wayne said, shuddering.

"Great." I plopped next to him on the sofa. "All we need to do now is find out who was recently in Australia."

"Starting with Mrs. Granger."

"It's lunch time," I said. "She's probably in the restaurant."

I led the way. Mom, my sister, Maryann, and my niece had already claimed a table. Angela took one look at Wayne and Dakota and shrieked. She launched herself at them, attracting the attention of everyone in the room. Maryann took one look at her brother and started to cry, then stumbled toward him, asking a million questions at once.

Cheri glared and held a finger to her lips.

I shrugged and headed to a back table where Amber sat staring at a plate of salad. "I've brought reinforcements."

"Good. Officer Rodriguez is breathing down my neck." She lifted a tear-filled gaze. "My Seth took a bath with jellyfish. Who would do that?" She put a hand to her head and pushed her coffee aside. "Something doesn't agree with me this morning."

I hoped it wasn't guilt as I introduced Matt as he sat next to me, leaving out the fact he was a detective. All Amber needed to know was that he was working as my partner.

"Have you been to Australia recently?" he asked.

She shook her head. "No, but Seth had. That's how I found out he was cheating. I found a pair of undies in his suitcase. How cliché is that? When I confronted him, he didn't deny my allegations and promised it wouldn't happen again."

"Did it?" Matt leaned forward, fixing his amazing chocolate stare on her.

"Not that I know of. I did not kill my husband, Mr.

Steele. I hired Miss Nelson to prove that fact."

So far, the widow knew as much about the case as I did.

Laughter erupted from a large table in the center of the room. The tiny veil on the head of one girl told me we had found the bridal party. I had an idea that Matt wouldn't like. At least I hoped he wouldn't, because it didn't taste good to me either. I dragged him away from Amber's table and out of sight.

"I want you to sit alone and make eyes at that table of women."

"Why?" He drew the word out.

"Because it's a bachelorette party, and you're a handsome man. I want you to cozy up to one of them and try to dig up some information."

"You're pimping me out." He grinned.

Okay, so he liked the idea more than I thought he would. "I guess."

"Can Wayne join me? He's good looking, too, right? At least, I've heard women say so."

"You'll have to take that up with Angela."

Ten minutes later, two very handsome men sat at a table next to the bevy of beauties while their girlfriends glowered from a table with their mother and teenagers.

"Stupid idea." Angela stabbed a piece of melon as if taking a stab at me. "I was excited about him being here and now…you've sent him undercover with younger women."

"Not one of them have your fake boobs, Mom." Cherokee shrugged. "You win."

I spewed orange juice onto my plate.

"What?" Cherokee glanced around. "Isn't that why Mom paid the big bucks? Because men like them?"

"For crying out loud!" Angela tossed her fork on the table and stormed from the restaurant, only to return seconds later. "I'm not letting that man out of my sight."

Mom chuckled and dug into her fruit salad. "Be yourself, dear. That's all any man worth his salt wants. I've seen the way Wayne looks at you. There's nothing to worry about." She glanced around the room. "If only there were some single men my age here."

"What are we doing today?" Dakota patted his stomach. "The food is great."

"I was thinking about a stroll through the garden," I said.

"How about a hike through the forest? The garden sounds lame."

"Let's do the forest tomorrow when we have more time," Mom suggested. "We can pack a lunch." She speared me with a glance. "You will come with us. I know you've said we'll solve this murder, and we will, but we're also going to have some fun."

No arguments there. We had a lot of heavy mental baggage to leave behind. Only fun and relaxation, along with lots of prayer, would accomplish that goal. I'd brought my laptop in case the inspiration to write struck me, but I didn't see that happening. Not with the activities and a new mystery. At least, death by jellyfish would provide a unique story line.

"Just great, Stormi." Angela thumbed over her shoulder. "The girls invited our men to their table. When Matt tells them he's suffering from a gunshot wound, they'll be all over him with giggles, caresses, and compassion. Wayne will be caught in the tow."

Good point. Maybe I should have rethought that idea.

I knew Matt loved me. Why else would he put up with all the trouble I got into in the name of research, but still…I gave an evil eye to one particular blond who had her arm around his good shoulder and was whispering in his ear. Maybe I should dump jellyfish in *her* bubble bath.

I immediately asked God for forgiveness for my unkind

thought and left the restaurant. My family followed.

The gardens lay to our right. With the beginning of fall, flowering blossoms were few and far between, but the changing foliage of autumn lit the area like a sunset. I chose an ornate iron bench and sat down, breathing deeply of air that didn't hold the stench of automobile exhaust or the wail of sirens. Not that Oak Meadows, the city I lived in, had a lot of that, but this place had none. True serenity. Until Angela opened her mouth.

"Why did you take the Granger murder job anyway? It isn't like you need the money. Aren't authors supposed to make up their stories? Writing books about other people's deaths is taking advantage of people's misfortune." She stood on her tiptoes. "I can't see in the restaurant window from here. Do you think Wayne is still there?"

"Where else would he be?" I closed my eyes and leaned my head back, wishing for earplugs. "Have some self-confidence." My thoughts weren't much different than hers, but if Matt looked elsewhere, he wasn't the man for me. Now, that thought actually hurt enough I opened my eyes.

The branch of a rosebush poked my side. I shoved it behind the bench and came face-to-face with my gardener. "Rusty!" I jumped up and yanked him from the bushes. "What are you doing here?"

"I came to watch over you." He dusted off the legs of his overalls. "I snuck in back of Matt's van." He grinned, showing blue teeth. "They have snow cones here."

"Does Matt know you're here?"

He shook his head. "I need vacation, too." He pointed at his leg. "No more crutches."

I sighed. The poor man had saved my mother's life, and most likely mine, a few weeks back. I couldn't send him away.

"He can sleep with me." Dakota clapped Rusty on the

shoulder. "I'll watch out for him."

"All we need now is Greta."

"I hope not," Mom said. "She's baking. We can't all go away or my business will falter."

Matt and Wayne, apparently escaping the clutches of their adoring new friends, strolled toward us. Matt's eyes widened at the sight of Rusty.

"He said he caught a ride with you." I cocked my head.

"I suppose. I didn't look in the back when I closed the door." He shrugged. "The more the merrier."

"I'm sure you thought so in the restaurant." I grimaced at my jealous remark.

He put his good arm around my waist and pulled me close so he could nuzzle my neck. "Don't worry. I did find out something, though."

I stepped back. "What?"

"One of the girls saw a woman going into cottage number twelve on the night of the murder." He grinned. "She said it wasn't Mrs. Granger, because that woman was having dessert, alone, in the restaurant."

"She could have left the restaurant."

"That's what I said. But, Lara said there was no way Amber could have made it past her at the time she saw the mystery woman. So…" he tapped my nose. "Chances are our killer is a woman."

"I'm thinking the woman Seth had an affair with." I bit the inside of my cheek. But who? There were at least twenty single women here, a few married ones, and even more on staff. It was a long list to work through.

"I don't suppose you can flirt and recoup with all the single ladies?"

"I won't go toying with hearts, Stormi."

"I know, it was a stupid idea. Where do we go from here?"

"I'll contact the airline and try to find out which days Seth flew to and from Australia, then post the list of other ticket buyers against the guest list here." He drew me close. "Let's head back and do some work."

"We'll stay here," Mom said. "Yell if you need us."

Angela had such a tight hold on Wayne's hand, he wasn't going anywhere either.

I had at least a few minutes alone with my honey. I snuggled against his side, frowning when he released me.

"If you want me to be able to get information from the single girls, we can't look like an item." He gave me a, "I'm sorry, but it was your idea" look.

Sometimes I was so stupid.

5

I plopped on the sofa and waited for Matt to join me when it felt safe. Mom entered the cottage and grinned.

"You're pouting like a child." She sat across from me. "Let's go over what we know about this murder. It'll take your mind off your jealousy."

Great idea. I tapped my finger on my lips. "Seth died by jellyfish. An unknown woman was seen entering his cottage. I'd ask about fingerprints, but I'm sure there are dozens. Amber's, the cleaning crew, Cheri's, the mysterious mistress." The suspect list was long and murky.

"Don't forget the window in the bathroom. The killer could have reached in, dumped the jellyfish, and be gone before Seth knew what was happening."

I straightened. "Was the window open?" For the life of me, I couldn't remember. I kept mine closed while taking my bath, and the shades drawn. Even with nothing behind the cottage but thick forest, I always felt vulnerable with bathroom windows. Wait. No, I hadn't. I'd taken my bath with the window open. A cool breeze had ruffled the curtains. I'd been so excited about the huge tub and done something completely out of character.

Mom shrugged. "I didn't go in. I'm assuming all the cottages are the same."

They probably were. I propped my feet on the table and

crossed my ankles. I tried to remember whether the Grangers' window had been open. I closed my eyes, envisioning a breeze. Nada. I'd seen the body and nothing else, other than a piece of octopus. But, to peer in the window, or drop something through it, a person would have needed a ladder. I made a mental note to check for marks in the dirt.

"It's disgusting." Maryann barged through the door and slumped next to me. "Wayne and my brother can't walk down the sidewalk without a bunch of giggling bimbos following them. What a dumb idea, Stormi."

"I'm starting to agree with you." The idea better pay off big time.

"It's like a piranha feeding frenzy out there." Matt rushed inside and slammed the door.

"Learning anything?" Maryann glowered and crossed her arms.

"A little." He squeezed between her and me. "Seems the Grangers didn't get along. The second honeymoon wasn't very sweet. They were heard screaming at each other earlier that evening."

"Things are not looking good for my client." I entwined my fingers with his.

"No, they're not. She had motive and opportunity."

"She didn't go to Australia, though."

"She says." He pulled some folded sheets of paper from his shirt. "This says differently." He spread the paper on the coffee table. "According to this…Amber arrived in Australia two days before Seth flew home. She took a flight back to the states the next morning."

"So, finding the underwear was a lie." I scanned the information. "She went there, saw him with another woman, purchased the jellyfish, and flew home with a vial of little killers." Three ounces or less in her purse wouldn't have raised suspicion. "We need to pay her another visit."

"You go with Anne. I need a break from those vultures." He gave me a quick kiss. "Be careful."

"We'll take our guns," Mom said, handing me my purse.

"I'll stay here and care for my brother." Maryann tried shoving a pillow behind his back. "You're recuperating, Matt. You shouldn't be doing anything with this case."

I agreed he shouldn't do too much, but it was nice having him on a case from the beginning rather than after I'd received death threats. "What did you tell those girls waiting outside about me?"

"I said you were my cousin." He grinned.

I wanted to hit him with the pillow that his sister kept trying to get him to use. Wonderful. We were on what could be a romantic getaway, and I had to pretend to be someone other than his fiancé. "If we're not back in an hour, call the cavalry."

The second floor of the main building had twelve single king-size bed suites. I stared at the doors lining the hall. "We should have asked which room Amber was in."

"Mrs. Granger is in room one-o-two," a maid said, exiting room one-o-one. "She's not feeling well."

"Thank you. We're checking on her." I knocked on Amber's door and waited for her to answer.

A pale, sweating version of the pretty woman peered through the opening. "Let me get the chain off." She fumbled for a moment, then opened the door. "Come in. I hope you don't mind talking to me while I lay down. I have a touch of the flu, I think."

She really did look awful, but I couldn't let my judgment be clouded by sympathy. I chose a chair by the small round table while Mom took the other.

Amber pulled the blankets up to her armpits. "I assume you're here to give me some news?"

"Actually," I leaned forward, balancing my elbows on my knees and peered intently into her eyes. "I want to know why you lied to me."

"Lied?" She paled further, if that were possible.

"You didn't find underwear in your husband's luggage. You went to Australia. Did you purchase the jellyfish there?"

She hung her head and took a shuddering breath. "I did find panties in the glove compartment of his car. I don't know how long they had been there, but…" She straightened. "that's why I flew to Australia. I caught him kissing a woman in the elevator of his hotel, and left before he could see me. I did not purchase anything. Not even a hotel room. I wandered Sydney until my flight the next day." Tears ran down her cheeks. "You have to believe me."

A check of credit card records should answer for sure. "Who is the woman?"

"I only saw the back of her head. She has blond hair."

So did half the population of the resort. "The facts are piling against you, Amber."

"Would I have hired you if I were guilty?"

"Maybe. If you thought hiring a PI would take the attention off of you."

"Despite his affair, I loved my husband. I need you to believe me." She turned green and made a dash for the bathroom.

The sound of retching had me making a beeline out of her room. Vomit and I did not get along. I leaned against the outside wall and took deep breaths while Mom, being the compassionate type, cared for Amber.

Despite overwhelming evidence to the contrary, I believed Amber's declaration of innocence. I'd made mistakes before in who to trust, but my gut told me she hadn't killed Seth. All I had to do was find the correct blond woman.

Three of the bridesmaids were blond, Cheri, two of the cleaning maids; those were the only the ones who came readily to mind. What if Seth's killer wasn't on the grounds? What if she'd made a special trip up the mountain for the sole purpose of dumping her tiny friends into his bubble bath? I had more questions than the SATs.

"You are such a baby," Mom said, joining me in the hall. "That is one sick girl. We need to check on her again in a couple of hours. She may need to see a doctor."

I nodded. "As long as you handle…that."

She narrowed her eyes. "How can you look at a dead body and see blood, but not stick around while someone is sick?"

"I have a phobia."

She shook her head. "You have a poor attempt at an excuse that you use at every opportunity. Now what?"

"Let's see if we can find that bevy of beauties who swarm around Matt and Wayne. Maybe we can do some eavesdropping or, if we're lucky, witness some suspicious behavior."

"You're grasping at straws."

"Yes, I am." I glanced down. "What is on your shoe? Oh, my, gosh." I staggered back. "Is that...is it…?"

"Oatmeal, Stormi. I dropped my breakfast. I guess I missed a spot when I cleaned up." She sighed and led the way to the elevator. "How did I raise such a child?"

I ignored her comment and headed for the pool area. The day held a definite nip in the air, but the pool was heated. Sure enough, the group huddled around the hot tub in bathing suits skimpy enough to barely be considered decent. In lounge chairs, reclined my fiancé and his partner. I scowled their way and chose seats away from them, but close enough to the hot tub that I could hear what the girls had to say.

Jealousy was not an experience I had been around much,

and I didn't like it a bit. Tears pricked the back of my eyelids. I needed to trust the man I loved. He was a good undercover detective. He would do his job and come back to me. As if he could read my thoughts, Matt winked my way, bringing my world back into focus.

"He is so hot!" A petite brunette glanced Matt's way.

I wanted to pull her hair out.

"A wounded cop. You can't get dreamer than that!"

"You're engaged, Shelby," one of the other girls said, giving Shelby a playful push. "Things didn't go so well when you fooled around with that married guy. He ended up dead."

My ears perked up so far, I probably looked like a rabbit. I glanced over and noticed a muscle ticking in Matt's jaw. He'd put on sunglasses and, to anyone looking at him, appeared to be sleeping.

"I didn't kill him, but how gross is that?" She clapped a hand over her mouth. "What if I was the last one to…you know…with him?"

"You didn't!"

She covered her face, but not before I saw her smile. "What happens at a bachelorette party stays at a bachelorette party. Besides, I'm tying the knot in a week. A girl needs to have some fun before going to prison."

"That's a sad way of looking at marriage."

"I'm only marrying him because of his money. He's old enough to be my father. He's the lucky one." She giggled and leaned back, her little white veil drifting on top of the water.

How could anyone go through life with that kind of a mindset? I wasn't a prude, by any means, but I'd made a vow in high school Sunday school class to wait until marriage. This woman did everything *but* wait. The mysteries I got involved in, sure showed the seedier side of life.

"If your groom finds out about you playing around, he'll

cancel the wedding."

"He won't find out." She wiggled her fingers at Wayne. "I don't leave a trail."

The blushing bride-to-be shot to the top of my suspect list. What if she killed Seth to keep him from spilling the beans about their little rendezvous?

6

"She's going to kill my Wayne." Angela stomped past me and wrapped her arms around Wayne's neck, then planted the steamiest kiss on his lips I'd ever seen outside of the movies. When she straightened, she sent a smug smile in the direction of the hot tub.

"Oh, honey, if I want your man, there isn't a thing you can do about it," Shelby said. "You remember that. But, if it's any consolation, I always throw my fish back."

Angela's face reddened, and her fists clenched. Mom took her by the arm and pulled her away before we had another murder on our hands.

I was torn between staying and keeping an eye on the women clearly interested in our men or helping Mom with my sister. I chose to leave. I wanted to google Shelby Richards.

On my way, I yanked Rusty from the bushes. "Stop spying. It's creepy."

"Rusty sees—"

"Yes, I know. Rusty sees things. Go get something to eat. Charge it to cottage ten." I continued to guide my sister away from the pool. Wait. "Rusty, what did you see?" When would I learn to listen to him?

"Mean girl."

"Yes. Several of them. You stay away, understand?"

He glanced toward the main building and nodded before dashing back to the bushes. A few seconds later, I spotted him scurrying through the door to the restaurant. His messages might be hard to decipher at times, but I was learning to listen when he spoke, sort of. At least, I was trying. I cast a glance back toward the pool area, then continued to the cottage.

"This is your fault!" Angela slapped me on the arm. "I'm going to lose him."

"Stop being so dramatic. If Wayne loves you, he won't go anywhere. We need him and Matt to flirt with these girls to see what they know." I shoved aside my own gnawing jealousy. "Instead, let's focus our attentions on finding out more about Bridezilla. Once this case is solved, you'll have Wayne back full time."

I carried my laptop to the round dinette table and booted it up. Typing in Shelby Richards brought up dozens of links. It seems our little bride made the rounds, appearing in several newspapers, attending charity functions, hanging on the arm of a handsome, but much older man. Further digging showed she didn't come from money. In fact, until being seen on a regular basis with multimillionaire Lawrence Boyd, she was unknown.

Little slutty, gold digger. I sat back and said a prayer of repentance. Who was I to judge her? I didn't know the path she'd had to walk through life. But...if she did kill Seth Granger, I would make sure she paid for the crime.

"I'm going to check on Amber. Anyone want to come with me?" Mom paused at the door.

"I'll come." I closed my laptop and followed, leaving my sister to continue her dramatics.

Shrill laughter and splashing came from the pool area. I sincerely hoped Matt wasn't romping in the water with those women. Everything in me wanted to go see. But, what little common sense I possessed at the moment said to let them be.

We took the elevator to the second floor and knocked on Amber's room. No one answered.

"Turn the knob," Mom said.

"We can't just barge in. What if she's in the shower?"

"As sick as she looked? No way." She reached around me and turned the knob. "Locked."

I rolled my head on my shoulders. "The doors lock automatically when closed, Mom."

"We need to get in that room. I have a bad feeling in my gut."

"You aren't catching whatever Amber has, are you?" I took a step back.

"Don't be ridiculous. I'm never sick. Wait here." She marched away.

I knocked again, louder and longer, then leaned against the wall to wait. Either Mom would return or Amber would open the door. Until then, I picked at my cuticles and tried to decide how to trip up the killer into making a wrong move. By the time Mom returned with Cheri, I had no idea how to proceed next.

"Are you sure she was ill enough this morning to warrant us entering her room uninvited?" Cheri frowned. "We try to respect the privacy of our guests."

"We're sure. Open the door, please." Mom gave a definitive nod.

The room reeked of one of the things I feared most in life…upchuck. I pinched my nose. "Amber?" I shared a worried look with Mom, then stepped further into the room.

Amber lay curled up on the bed in her vomit.

"Stay there." Mom stepped next to the bed and felt for a pulse. "She's dead."

I dug my cell phone out of my pocket with my free hand and called Matt. "I need you. Main building. Second floor.

Hurry."

"Be right there." Click.

My next call was to the police.

Mom pulled up the bed sheet and covered Amber, before doing the grossest thing I've ever seen anyone do. She leaned close and smelled the throw up. "Did Amber smoke?"

I shrugged. "I've never seen evidence of it," I said, nasally, slowly backing from the room until I found my way blocked by a heavy breathing Matt.

"Whoa." His hands on my shoulders steadied me. "What is that smell?"

I pointed and continued backing from the room as Wayne rushed in. At the end of the hall was the bridal party.

"What's going on?" Shelby marched toward me, her eyes grew wide, and she froze. "Oh, my…" She gagged and joined her friends.

Wayne marched from the room and back to the girls. "Nothing to see here, ladies. Go on back to the pool."

They tried to peer around him, to no avail. Wayne made evasive moves worthy of any NFL player.

"What happened?" Shelby planted her fists on her hips. "As a guest here, I demand to know why you can go in and I can't."

Because you're a spoiled brat, is what I was thinking, but wisely kept my mouth shut and watched Wayne try to corral a bevy of curious women. Under different circumstances, I would have found the show very entertaining

Officer Rodrigues stormed down the hall alongside two paramedics. He glanced at me and shook his head. "You're like a virus."

I've been called worse. I moved back to Amber's doorway, hearing things like poison and murder. Why would someone want to kill her? Her cheating husband—I could understand—but Amber seemed sweet and forgiving, despite being a liar.

"Shelby." A loud voice boomed down the hallway.

I turned and spotted none other than the unhappy groom-to-be stepping into the middle of the bridal party.

"It's time for you to come home. This resort is a dangerous place."

Matt shot past me. "I'm afraid that can't happen, sir. Shelby Richards is a suspect in a murder investigation. We're asking all the guests to stay here, if possible, until the investigation is complete."

Lawrence Boyd turned and glared. "What constitutes *im*possible to stay?"

"Death in the family." Matt met his stare. "I'm Detective Steele. This is my partner, Detective Jones, and Officer Rodrigues from the local police station. We're in charge of the investigation. Feel free to stay with your fiancée if you must, but she isn't going anywhere." He turned and marched back to Amber's room.

I loved that man. He managed with a few words to put one of the most influential men in Arkansas in his place.

"Why are you a suspect?" Lawrence turned on Shelby.

"I don't know. They must hate me because I'm marrying you. Those officers haven't had a problem flirting with me until now. If you knew the things they've asked me to do." She wrapped around his arm. "Come to the cottage."

"Things I've no doubt you weren't willing to do. I've reserved a room for the two of us on this floor. I had hoped to leave in the morning. Now, that cannot happen." He pulled free. "What did you do, Shelby?"

Cheri exited Amber's room. "Everyone should leave. Go to your rooms. If the authorities need to speak with you, then they will come to you." She held out her hand to Lawrence. "Nice to meet you, Mr. Boyd. I'm the manager of this resort. Let me know if I can do anything to make your stay more pleasant."

"You can start with telling me why Shelby is being detained."

"You poor dear." She flicked a glance at Shelby. "Your fiancée has been rather, well, to put it delicately, unfaithful. With the man who is now dead. Please, enjoy your stay." She glided down the hall as if she hadn't a care in the world.

I scratched my head. While the entertainment in the hall was riveting, I wanted to know what was happening in Amber's room. Instead, I plastered myself against the opposite wall as Lawrence marched his naughty fiancée to room number five. The man looked angry enough to kill.

Could he have found out about her dalliance with Seth and taken out the competition? But, that didn't give him a motive to kill Amber, if she had, indeed, been murdered.

Matt looked out of the room. "You can leave. I'll come to the cottage when I've finished here and showered."

I blew him a kiss and grabbed Mom's arm. "What did you see in there?"

"The same thing you saw, only I didn't run out like a rabbit. That poor girl. What an awful way to die."

"How do you think she died?"

"Remember that police drama episode we saw a while back where the man killed his wife by nicotine poisoning?"

I gasped. "You think?"

"She had the symptoms, and her vomit smelled a lot like an ashtray. There wasn't a single thing in that room to show she smoked. I think it's a strong possibility."

Seth died by jellyfish poisoning and, now, Amber by nicotine. One which is difficult to acquire, the other very easy.

I needed to find a way to get into Shelby's room.

7

"**Y**ou have to get that master key card," Mom said, blowing on a mug of hot coffee. "I'm sure there are more than the one Cheri carries."

The trick will be getting into the office again. I doubt I could be that lucky twice, and Mom's silly diversion about a cougar on the grounds wouldn't work again.

"Are we going hiking at all on this so-called vacation?" Cherokee plopped next to me.

"First thing after breakfast tomorrow. I promise." I rested my head on the back of the sofa. "How are you at stealing?"

She shrugged. "I'm okay at it. I took stuff from Mom's purse all the time when I was little. What do you want me to steal?"

"You did what?" Angela glared from the chair opposite us. "No wonder I never had any money."

"This is different than taking twenty dollars out of your Mom's purse. I need Cheri's master key card."

"Oh, that will be easy. One of the busboys in the restaurant has the hots for me. I'll just tell him she confiscated something of mine and I need a card to get it back."

I shook my head. "Too risky. I don't want to involve a third party."

"I got it!" Mom tapped her temple. "Always thinking, I

am. I was in the restroom in the atrium and Cheri walked in. She hangs her card on a hook next to the sink. All you have to do is follow her until she goes in there. Voila!"

I closed my eyes and rubbed my temple. "That's one of your craziest ideas. If she knows the card is missing, she'll change it."

"Let's hear your great idea." Mom frowned.

"I don't have one. That's why we're brainstorming."

"I'm telling you to leave it to me." Cherokee pushed to her feet. "I'll be back in fifteen minutes. A girl has to have *some* fun on vacation."

I glanced at Angela, who shrugged. "Okay, if it's all right with your mother—"

She grinned. "Be right back with the card."

"She's an adult now." Angela sighed. "She doesn't need my permission."

"Maybe not," Mom said, "but it's nice when they ask." She sent me a pointed look.

"What?" I held up my hands.

"Nothing. So, which room do we search first? The bridal party cottage or Shelby and her foolish groom?"

I thought for a moment. "Both, but the cottage first. I doubt she'll move any incriminating evidence to the room she shares with Lawrence. He doesn't strike me as a dumb man." Rather smart, in fact. Which made his putting up with Shelby's shenanigans all the more confusing. Could she have something to hold over his head that could ruin him financially or his standing in the community? We'd definitely find the time to check both places.

"Ta-da!" Cherokee burst in and dropped a plastic key card on the coffee table. "I didn't have to do anything. This card was lying on the front desk next to the computer."

I wondered who it belonged to. It was possible the card had been wiped clean, but since it had the words 'Master' printed on the front, it was worth a try. "Mom, come with me and be the lookout."

Cherokee huffed. "Why can't I come? I stole the key."

"And I feel terrible about turning you into a thief. I don't want to add breaking and entering to my faults as an aunt." I stuck the card under my bra strap. "Why don't you do some digging on the computer. Research the Grangers and Shelby Richards. Lawrence, too, if you have time. If you find something interesting, I'll pay you twenty dollars."

"Deal!" She sat in front of my laptop as Mom and I left.

We turned right toward the bridal cottage. A quick glimpse into the restaurant window confirmed the cottage was empty. The gals drank mimosas like water.

"This is the kind of mystery I don't mind solving," Mom said, taking up her position next to the door.

"How so?" I slid the card into the slot in the door.

"We haven't been in danger once."

I enjoyed that aspect, myself. "Whistle if someone comes." The light in the slot glowed green, and I opened the door. The place, decorated the same as our cottage, looked as if a tornado had blown through. Women's clothing was draped over every available surface and puddled on the floor. I pitied the maid service.

"You know I can't whistle."

"Then make bird calls." I closed the door, but not far enough for the lock to engage.

Eight, well, now seven, women occupied the space. That put three in each room. Which one Shelby had stayed in was anybody's guess. I entered the one on my right first. It had more clothes strewn around than the living room. This was going to take a while.

I opened every drawer, looked in every cabinet, and in every trash can. Nada. I wasn't sure what I was looking for, but whatever it was, I wasn't finding it. No vials of sea water or containers of nicotine. No gun, knife, or other such weapon. I perched on the edge of one of the beds. I'd even snooped in six makeup bags and found nothing more deadly than a pair of cuticle scissors.

"Caw, caw!"

I exhaled sharply at Mom's attempt to make a bird call. I hurried to the door and slipped outside seconds before being spotted by the bridal party.

A tall brunette scowled. "What are you doing outside of our cottage?"

"Your cottage. I thought—" I peered at the number next to the door. "My bad. We have the wrong cottage." At least the place was such a mess, they'd never know someone had been snooping inside.

"Find anything?" Mom glanced over her shoulder as we strode toward the main building.

"Just a mess. If Shelby is the guilty party, she either disposed of the evidence or took it with her."

"I haven't seen hide nor hair of her or her fiancé. What do we do if they stay holed up in their room?"

"Maybe we can think of a reason for Matt to interrogate them somewhere other than their room." Of course, with nothing to go on but suspicions, that wasn't likely.

"Tonight is the semi-formal get together. If they come out of their room, that will be the time."

I agreed, and I couldn't wait to put on a pretty dress and lay claim to my man in front of the bridal gals. Being outside Amber's room earlier let them know Matt wasn't a regular guest. With no need for any such pretense anymore, it wouldn't hurt to let everyone know we are an item.

We changed course and headed back to our cottage where Matt waited, asleep on the sofa, and Wayne cuddled with a very happy Angela. I stared down at my honey, regretting the fact he was spending his recuperation time knee-deep in a murder. It remained a mystery why such a man loved a woman who attracted trouble, yet he did.

He cracked open an eye and smiled, holding a hand out to me. "Lay with me."

I grinned and spread out next to him, eagerly awaiting the time we could do this every night, without my giggling sister sitting a few feet away. "Have a nice rest?" I caressed his cheek. Stubble rasped against my palm.

"A little. Where were you?"

"Snooping in the bridal party cottage. Didn't find a thing."

"Okay. This room has gotten too gross." Cherokee sat in the bend of my knees and squirmed to find enough room to sit. "You owe me twenty bucks."

I struggled to a sitting position. "What did you find out?"

"Seth Granger used to work for Boyd Industries as an accountant. Guess who his secretary was? Yep! Shelby Richards. Seth quit working there last year, no reason why, and Shelby started cozying up to Lawrence. What do you want to bet that Seth found out something about Lawrence that needed hushing up?" She held out her hand.

"Good job." I fished a twenty from my purse. "Now, we need to find out exactly why Seth quit Boyd Industries. We need back in Amber's room." I turned to Matt. "Can you get us past the yellow tape?"

He laughed. "Like that's ever stopped you before. But, yes, I can. Rodriguez has asked for mine and Wayne's unofficial help on these murders." He got to his feet and helped me up. "Let's go snooping. Your favorite pastime."

"Doubly so when I'm going with you."

With our fingers entwined, we headed to the second floor of the main building and ducked under the yellow crime scene tape strung across Amber's door. I bet that sent shivers up and down Cheri's spine every time she had to see the reminder of bad publicity.

Matt handed me a pair of rubber gloves. "I know this is probably futile. You and your mother most likely touched everything in here."

A good part. Oh, why hadn't someone taken care of the stench? "How do you breathe?"

"I've smelled worse." He pulled a wrinkled paper mask from his pocket. "A gift."

"I love you." I couldn't put it on fast enough. It didn't alleviate the smell, but it did fade it some. Enough, at least, that I could tolerate being in the room. I left the gross side of the room to Matt and headed for Amber's suitcases. From the tossed clothing, something I hadn't seen evidence of when Amber was alive, someone had already dug through her things. What were they looking for and had they found it?

I emptied the suitcase, ignoring Matt's grunts of disapproval. I wrote mysteries. I knew things were not always what they seemed. After several seconds of careful feeling, I found it. A false bottom. "Matt."

He peered over my shoulder. "Clever girl. That's why I love you."

"The only reason?"

"Nah, you're pretty."

I lifted the bottom to reveal several sheets of printed pages. "Let's get these back to the cottage and look through them. Should we put the suitcase back together?"

"Nope. I want the killer to know we're on to them. Hopefully, it will flush them out of hiding." He tweaked my nose. "Just don't drink any coffee you didn't prepare yourself and no bubble baths."

"That, my dear, is a bad joke." I grabbed the papers and followed Matt out the door. Outside, I removed the mask and shoved it in my pocket. A girl never knew when she might need one.

"I feel like we've won the lottery." I did a little jig.

"Feeling frisky today, Miss Nelson?" Cheri gave a smile that didn't quite reach her eyes. "Since you visited poor Mrs. Granger's room, I was hoping you would give the all clear so we could clean it and resume business as usual."

My good mood evaporated. "It's all about the mighty dollar to you, isn't it?" I frowned.

She shrugged and sighed. "I have a job to do. One I'm very good at." Her smile returned. "Well?"

"I'll speak to Officer Rodriguez," Matt said. "I'm sure we can release the room soon."

"Thank you." She laid a hand on his arm. "You're a kind man. Let me know if there is anything you need. Don't forget our semi-formal dinner and dance tonight"

She strolled away, leaving me as if I'd been in the presence of a shark.

"Creepy." She might look like a fashion model, but there was definitely something off about the resort's manager.

"Dinner and dance?" Matt's face paled. "I didn't bring anything to wear to that."

I laughed and tugged him toward a boutique I'd spotted next to the gift shop. "Let me buy you a suit."

8

I slipped into the little black dress I'd packed and put my hair in a stylish French twist. A slab of scarlet lipstick, my feet in strappy black sandals, and I was ready for a night out with my man. I couldn't wait to see him in the charcoal suit I'd bought him. He'd fussed, but I saw his eyes light up when he spotted it hanging on the rack. Why did most men make a big deal about a woman purchasing something for them?

Matt stood in the living room, and he was worth every cent, even with his arm in a sling. Wheat-colored hair slicked back from his handsome face. Just a trace of stubble on his strong cheeks, and those amazing chocolate-colored eyes. Be still my heart.

"You look beautiful," I said.

"If I look half as amazing as you do, then I'm happy to be wearing a monkey suit. A very nice one, by the way. Thank you." He crooked his arm. "Ready? The others will meet us in the ballroom."

"The resort has a ballroom?" Fancy.

"Yep. We even managed to get your nephew into dress clothes."

"This I have to see."

The night carried a slight chill. Another reminder that fall was settling in. Vapor rose from the heated pool and hot tub, lending a mysterious air to the evening. A cloudless sky formed the perfect backdrop for millions of stars. The evening couldn't be more romantic.

One glimpse through the door of the ballroom told me it could. Every guest must have decided to attend. A romantic evening would be alone time with Matt. Instead, I plastered on a smile, gripped Matt's arm tighter, and sailed through the throng toward the large round table my family had confiscated.

Sure enough, Dakota wore a burgundy dress shirt and tie with dark washed blue jeans. Dressed up for my skateboarding nephew. Cherokee was in a simple spaghetti strapped dress that shimmered with blues and purples when she moved. Angela, was barely dressed in a dress that matched my lipstick. Maryann was sunny in a golden gown that flounced at the knee. Mom had opted for a royal blue sheath dress. Wayne looked uncomfortable in a navy suit.

"My, we clean up nice." I hung my purse on the back of my chair and slid onto the seat Matt pulled out for me.

"Isn't this lovely." Mom smiled. "A catered dinner and dancing. Too bad I'm a single wheel."

"I'll dance with you, Grandma." Dakota patted her hand. "It's better than dancing with my sister."

"Shut up." Cherokee rolled her eyes. "As if I'd dance with a fungus like you." She smiled at her camera and took a selfie. Her smile turned to a pout the moment after she snapped the picture. "This whole night is lame. This whole vacation is lame." She sighed as if life was horrible and propped her chin in the palm of her hand. "We need more action."

I sincerely hoped she didn't mean of the murderous type. "We're hiking tomorrow."

"Oh, goody. Maybe we'll see a bear." Sarcasm dripped from her words.

"Be careful what you wish for." My attention diverted to the entrance where Shelby, gorgeous is a form-fitting dress of ice blue, hung on Lawrence's arm. She looked every bit the happy bride-to-be. Unfortunately for her, I'd seen her dark side.

She flashed a grin toward our table, and motioned for, I'm guessing Matt or Wayne, to call her. I groaned and shook my head. The woman was shameless. "Didn't she hear you say she was a murder suspect? She knows you're both cops."

"I doubt she cares." Matt shrugged out of his jacket and hung it on the back of his chair. "If she gets me in her clutches, I wonder what I might get poisoned with."

"That's too scary to contemplate."

Servers in white jackets set bowls of bread on each table, then made the rounds with small plates of salad. In a far corner, a band tuned their instruments. From the age of the members, I guessed we'd be hearing easy listening songs very soon.

I poured a cranberry vinaigrette on my salad and wondered what had gone so wrong with a couple of weeks intended to help us get over the horror of Cherokee's abduction. Why couldn't I go anywhere, do anything, without running into a murder? Was this my fate in life? What about when I was old? Was I the future Miss Marples?

"Why so serious?" Matt peered into my face. "It's a party."

"Just thinking. Have you ever wondered how I get into these messes? All. The. Time?"

"You're talented." He kissed the tip of my nose. "I've come to accept it."

I bumped him with my shoulder. "Very funny."

The next course was filet with parmesan crusted asparagus as a side. Yum! The fact the meal was included in our cost added to the flavor.

"Is everything to your liking?" Cheri stopped, placing a hand on Matt's shoulder. "We want your stay here to be very pleasant." She glanced at me. "You may pick up your packed lunch in the restaurant kitchen before your hike."

"Thank you."

"And, Miss Nelson? Please take your friend with you." She motioned her head to where Rusty hovered in the doorway, wearing his overalls and a red bow tie with white polka dots. "I'm getting complaints about him." She took a deep breath and moved to the next table.

I waved for Rusty to join us. He glanced at Cheri, seemed to wait until she'd moved another table away, then joined us, pulling up an empty chair. "That woman yelled at me."

"Just stay away from her, pal." Matt clapped him on the shoulder. "We're going hiking in the morning. Come with us."

He nodded. "I'll keep the bears away." He pulled a whistle from his pocket and put it to his lips. The shrill sound turned everyone's frowning attention our way.

"That'll work." Matt pulled it away from Rusty's lips. "Save it for the woods."

Rusty finished off the bread in the basket, his salad, then his dinner in that order and quicker than I've ever seen anyone eat. When finished, he belched, wiped his hands on his overalls, and limped quickly from the table to "keep an eye on things" or so he said.

I hoped Cheri wasn't too rough on him. He meant well.

By the time we'd finished dinner and started on a cherry chocolate cheesecake, the band started playing. Matt took my hand and pulled me onto the dance floor and into a foxtrot that took us to the other side. "Do you mind if we mosey closer to the lovebirds?"

Shelby and Lawrence conversed in quiet tones, heads together, as they swayed to the music. Through another door,

I spotted Rusty spying through the leafy branches of a silk ficus tree.

"Tell me you had nothing to do with Seth Granger's death," Lawrence asked Shelby.

She peered up at him. "I promise. We had nothing but a fling."

"For over a year." He gave her a grin without humor. "I'm not sure how much longer I can tolerate your infidelities. I have grand plans for my future. I need a wife above reproach."

"I can be that wife, dear." She planted a heavy kiss on his lips. "No one stirs your blood as I do. Don't worry. No one will ever find out what Seth knew about Boyd Industries. I've destroyed any evidence left behind."

Except several sheets of paper stashed in a dead woman's suitcase. Once Matt and I figured out what they meant, a certain slutty bride was going to jail for murder.

Matt twirled me past them. "We don't want to make them suspicious."

"I'm the one who's suspicious. She all but confessed."

"She did say some incriminating things, but we still have time to determine whether she's the killer or not." He put a finger on my lips to stop my protest. "Oh, she's guilty, sweetheart. I'm just not exactly sure of what. Can we sit? Dancing the foxtrot with a bum arm is painful."

"Yes, but you owe me at least one slow dance."

"You got it."

"I'm glad Rusty is going hiking with us," Dakota said the moment we sat down. "I was talking to him earlier about our favorite television shows, and he likes Discovery and National Geographic. He knows a lot about bears and cougars." He sipped a Dr. Pepper. "For bears, you have to make a lot of noise. If it's a brown bear, you play dead. If it's a black bear, you pretend to be bigger than you are. They're actually scared of us. Cougars…well, they won't attack a large group, but will stalk if a person is alone."

"He said all that?" I plopped onto my seat. "In complete sentences?"

He looked taken aback. "He talks all the time, Aunt Stormi. All you have to do is listen. He snores like a train, though. Don't ever share a room with him."

I laughed. "I'll remember that."

A screeching came from the direction I'd last spotted Rusty. With Matt on my heels, I rushed that way in time to see Shelby wagging a finger in Rusty's face.

"I swear, you idiot, if you don't stop spying on me, you'll meet the same fate as the Grangers!"

"That's enough." Matt pulled her away and thrust her toward Lawrence, who was just joining us. "Control her, or I will lock her up."

"Some women can't be controlled, Officer." Lawrence put his arm around Shelby's shoulders. "I like her spirited."

"Spirited and mean are two separate things. Come on, Rusty. It's time for you to go back to the cottage."

"And don't drink anything you don't prepare for yourself," I whispered. My gardener might be tough to keep an eye on, but I definitely didn't want him dead.

"Do I have to boil my water?" Rusty rubbed between his eyes.

"What? No. Don't drink anything unless Matt or I check it out first. And for heaven's sake, don't take a bath."

"Shower?"

"Yes, please." I cast an imploring look at Matt. "I think our evening is over. I don't want him left alone tonight."

"All right." He pulled me close for a kiss. "We'll meet you by the pool in the morning. I love you."

"I love you, too." Darn that Shelby Richards. I stomped my foot and headed outside. Maybe some cool air would calm my temper.

I wrapped my arms around me in an attempt to ward off a chill and headed for the pool. I could stick my feet in the hot tub and stay warm while I mulled over in my mind the best way to bring Shelby to her knees. With handcuffs on her wrists, preferably. Violence wasn't my forte when riled, but I wanted to slap her at that moment.

The sound of sobbing reached me before I stepped through the open pool gate. Dangerous. I hadn't spotted any young children at the resort, but wasn't a closed gate mandatory for public places? I pulled the gate closed.

Cheri sat on a lounge chair, bent over, sobs shaking her body. When she spotted me, she darted out of sight.

9

It took two backpacks to carry enough food for a picnic the size of my group. One of the busboys helped me put one on my shoulders, then I hefted the other one in my arms and made my way to the cottage. All before six a.m. the next morning.

This was insane. Who woke up this early on vacation?

Luckily for me, Rusty and Wayne volunteered to wear the packs, despite Matt's argument that he didn't need two arms to wear something on his back. My poor baby. I patted his cheek on my way to the bedroom.

Eyeing my purse, I decided against my gun. I'd seen Matt's and Wayne's in their shoulder holsters. Two guns were probably one too many on a simple hike.

Mary Ann tied laces on a pair of hiking boots. "Sorry I haven't been much help with this mystery. It's just been so long since I've had any recreation time."

"I understand. Technically, with Amber dead, I'm no longer employed by her. I can let the whole thing drop and let the cops handle it from here." I pulled a long sleeved T-shirt over the short sleeve one I wore. Layering was important, right?

"Can you let it go?" She stood.

"I can try. But, Matt is helping Rodriguez, and I'm helping Matt." I grinned.

"Make all the excuses you want, but someday, your guardian angel is going to throw his hands in the air and you'll be on your own." Her expression grew grave. "I enjoy the successes as much as you do. Really. But, you need to learn to relax."

"I didn't ask for this."

"No, but you accepted the case. Have you even looked at the papers you took from Amber's suitcase?"

"Yes. It's just a bunch of numbers. Matt is having someone at the precinct go over them." I crossed my arms, hurt by her lack of support. "See? I can let the authorities handle things."

"I just don't want you to collapse because you never take a break. Come on. Let's go exhaust ourselves with something healthy."

We joined the group in the courtyard where Mom took control immediately. "No one ventures from the path. Remember the saying, 'take only pictures, leave only footprints'. There is no need to be aggressively loud." she shot a stern look at Rusty, who had his hand on his whistle. "We'll make enough noise with a group this size to scare away anything. There are rock bridges and caves to see. Let's enjoy the day." She grabbed a walking stick propped against the cottage and set off at a brisk pace toward the trail.

"I want a walking stick," I said. "Where did you get it?"

"I got you one from the gift shop." Matt pulled one from behind a bush. "Somehow, I knew the green dragon of jealousy would rear his head."

"Thanks!" I gripped the polished oak stick. "I'm ready."

The day couldn't be more gorgeous. Just enough of a chill to make the air seem fresher. A thin veil of fog hung over the mountains in the distance. Birds chirped from the trees. The sun dappled the path ahead of us. It was a perfect day.

I slipped my free hand in Matt's good one and followed the group down the trail.

"What time are we going to eat?" Dakota opened a water bottle. "I'm starved."

A whistle split the air. "Hey, Bear!" Rusty yelled.

I jumped and clapped a hand to my chest. "Do not do that again."

"We're entering the forest," he said, as if I were stupid.

"Can we just enjoy nature?"

"Not if you're eaten." He pointed at a small sign stuck in the dirt. "It says to call out for the bear."

Good point. "Then, stand in front so you don't frighten me to death." There goes any chance at all of seeing wildlife.

"Is no one going to answer me about lunch?" Dakota held out his hands.

"Here." Mom tossed him a granola bar. "This hike will take several hours. At the halfway point, we'll eat."

"Hours?" Angela glanced at the stylish gym shoes on her feet. "Will these hold up that long?"

The morning grew warmer. I pulled off my long sleeved tee and tied the arms around my waist. I refused to let the others' complaints ruin the day. The brochure clearly stated it was a day long hike through some of the Ozark's most beautiful scenery. Then, we could do another massage tomorrow to work out the sore muscles.

Rusty blew his whistle again. "Hey, Bear!"

For crying out loud. "I'm going to ram that whistle down your throat." I immediately felt bad when he gave me a wounded look. Lord, help us. "I'm sorry. I know you're only trying to protect us."

"I heard back on the papers from Amber's suitcase," Matt said.

"You're just now telling me?"

"I heard late last night. Do you want to know or not?"

"Of course, I do."

"They are a bunch of fake companies and bank account numbers. The numbers are real. The companies are not. Whoever supposedly has these accounts is a very wealthy person by dishonest means."

"Do you think they belong to Boyd Industries?"

"It crossed my mind." He held his finger to his lips. "Don't mention it to anyone. The only other person who knows is Wayne."

I nodded. If we found out who the accounts belonged to, we could very well have our killer. We needed to find out soon. Our rooms were rented for one more week. I didn't want to fork over more funds to stay longer. Not when I had a perfectly good Victorian house, a dog, and two cats waiting for me.

We eventually stopped at a flat ledge of rock that overlooked a tree-filled canyon. Reds, yellows, and oranges erupted in a blinding display of autumn. Mom planted her hands on her hips and declared we were having lunch because someone's stomach was growling a bit loudly.

We glanced around at each other. Then, I heard the growl. It was not a stomach. I gripped Matt's good arm. "What was that?"

"Get behind me."

Rusty blew long and hard on his whistle.

Wayne ripped it from the string around the other man's neck and tossed the whistle over the ledge.

A bear poked its head through the thick brush and roared.

Cherokee wrapped her arms around her brother's neck.

Angela screamed as Wayne thrust her behind him.

"I'll get some food for it out of the backpack," Mom said, slowly moving behind Wayne. She unzipped the pack and reached inside to pull out something bleeding through butcher paper. "Who would put raw meat in here?"

"Someone who wanted one of us dead." I grabbed the steak and tossed it at the bear. "Everyone back slowly down the path."

Matt and Wayne took the walking sticks and stayed between the bear and the rest of us.

"Shoot it!" Tears ran down Cherokee's face.

"That will only make it angrier."

"It's wounded," Dakota said. "Isn't that a knife sticking out of its shoulder?"

I could be jumping to conclusions, but it sure looked like someone had gone to great personal danger to make sure we were stalked by an enraged bear. Angela screamed again and took off down the trail. The others followed, leaving Matt, Wayne, and myself facing an animal standing on its hind legs pawing at the air.

"You're going to have to shoot it," Matt told Wayne. "With a handgun. Don't miss and don't stop until you're out of bullets."

"A shame. Beautiful animal." He pulled his gun from his shoulder holster and started firing as the bear charged.

With another roar, it swiped at him, catching Wayne in the shoulder and spinning him. His foot slipped in loose leaves and he fell.

Matt shrugged free of his arm sling and swung the walking stick like a baseball bat.

The bear turned.

"Hey!" I picked up a fist sized rock and bounced it off the bear's head. "Don't let me die, Wayne. Shoot it!" I took off running as fast as I could.

Shots rang out behind me.

"Stormi."

I turned at Matt's call.

The bear lay at Wayne's feet. Blood soaked Wayne's shirt and Matt's face was etched in pain.

The others trickled back and stared down at what had once been a magnificent black bear.

"Who would do this?" Mom petted the animal as if it could feel her gentle touch. Maybe it could somehow.

I glared at Angela. "You know better than to scream and run with a bear. Now, take care of your man while I tend to mine."

"I'm sorry." She hung her head. "I don't think well when I'm frightened."

Rusty kneeled beside the bear and yanked out the knife before anyone could stop him. "This came from the restaurant."

"Are you sure?" Matt froze with his arm halfway in the sling.

Rusty nodded. "I watched man carve ham yesterday."

"How did someone get the knife in the bear without the bear killing them?" None of it made sense. I untied my shirt from around my waist and handed it to Angela to bind Wayne's shoulder.

"Someone with a good throwing arm might have succeeded." Matt glanced down the trail. "Maybe we had company today and didn't know it until it was too late." He glanced up into the trees. "If someone sat in a tree and dropped a very sharp knife at the right moment, it could have penetrated the bear's skin, maybe. I'm speculating here."

"Do you think they were hoping one of us would wander off?" I wrapped my arms around my waist at the sudden chill.

"My guess is that someone wanted you. All they would have had to do was wait until you stepped off the trail to take care of business."

"Why me?" Why was it always me?

Maryann sighed. "I told you. It's because you don't know how to say no to a murder investigation."

It was a very good thing I had limited my water on the hike. I glanced back at the poor animal. That could very well have been me lying there with a knife in my back.

63

10

Wayne held up like a trooper, but by the time we arrived back at the resort, he could barely stand from pain and loss of blood. The moment we were able to get cell phone reception, we'd called to have an ambulance waiting. Paramedics met us thirty minutes from the end of the hike.

They bandaged Wayne's shoulder, belted him to a stretcher, and bounced him the rest of the way into an ambulance.

"I'm going with him." Matt gave me a quick kiss. "I pulled some stitches that will need a doctor to take care of. I'll call and let you know how he's doing as soon as I can."

I nodded and swallowed against the tears. Only I could put my family in danger on a hike.

"I know what you're thinking," Mom said. She stepped to my right, and Maryann to my left. "You're thinking this is somehow your fault. It isn't. Not unless you stabbed that bear and put a raw steak in the backpack. Did you?"

I shook my head, a half-sob, half-laugh escaping. "That takes a truly twisted mind."

"The same mind that kills with jellyfish and nicotine," Maryann added. "I think I will help you with this case after all. It's too much for you, even with my brother helping. You need twenty-four hour surveillance. Since I share a room with you, that leaves me to be your bodyguard."

"You're getting plenty of experience." I turned back to our cottage as the ambulance pulled away.

"Miss Nelson," Cheri called. "Let me know if there is anything I can do. I promise to get to the bottom of the steak in the backpack. You can count on that with all certainty."

I whirled. "Who told you there was a steak in the pack?"

She took a step back. "I overheard one of the detectives talking." She clapped a hand over her mouth. "I'm sorry. Was that a secret?"

"You might not want it spread around that your kitchen staff is so careless." I continued away from her. The hairs on the back of my neck prickled.

I stopped and surveyed the crowd. One of them was a killer. It could be one of the shocked, and for once, silent bridesmaids. The bride or groom. Or someone I had yet to put a name to. Whether I'd met the killer or not, he, or she, was watching and gloating.

I called out to Cheri before she disappeared out of sight. "I couldn't help but see you were upset last night. Is there anything I can do to help?"

"No, thank you." Her smile wavered. "I recently lost someone dear to me. I'll be all right. It's just that all this…death, brings the memories to mind." She entered the main building, pulling the doors tight. Her gaze never left mine. I was the first to turn away.

"It was quite an endeavor," I said, entering the cottage and sliding the chain on the door behind me. "The killer couldn't know for sure I would be the one harmed."

"Maybe the person didn't care. It could be a warning that you're getting too close." Maryann sat on one end of the sofa, brought her knees up and hugged a throw pillow. "The thing that makes me extremely nervous is that we don't know where the next attack is coming from."

Angela entered the room, dragging her suitcases behind

her. "Forget that we paid for the next week. I want to go home."

"Sit down, dear, and be quiet." Mom measured coffee grounds. "You don't want to go anywhere with Wayne in the hospital now, do you?"

She slumped in a chair. "No, but I'm worried for my kids."

"I'm an adult," Cherokee said quietly. "I say we see this thing through. It's personal now."

"Are you sure?" I studied her expressionless face. "We came so you could relax and let *the ordeal* stay behind you. If this is too much, we'll go home. No questions asked, no arguments."

Every head turned to look at her. Even Rusty glanced up from the table where he ate cookies from one of the packs. A person could have heard a pin drop.

A knock sounded on the door.

I jumped.

Angela screamed.

Mom grabbed her purse. "Where's my gun?"

"Dakota, hand me my purse." He handed me my Glock.

"That's what you really wanted, right?"

I nodded and slowly made my way to the door. A peek between the curtains had me relaxing for a second, before I remembered they often sent police officers to someone's house to inform them of a loved one's death. I yanked the door open. "Yes?" I stared up at Officer Rodriguez.

"May I come in?"

"Do you bring bad news?"

I couldn't see his eyes behind mirrored sunglasses, but he cocked his head. "Excuse me?"

"Yes, come in." I stepped aside. This day was not getting better. "Have a seat."

"I'll stand." Although, he did remove his sunglasses.

"I've already spoken to Detectives Steele and Jones. But, I'd like to hear what happened from the rest of you."

"It charged out of nowhere!"

"It tried to eat us, I swear."

"We ran as fast as we could."

"Mom screamed and made the bear mad."

My family and friends all spoke at once.

Officer Rodrigues put two fingers in his mouth and whistled sharply. "One at a time. Miss Nelson, you first, since you were the only one not talking."

He might choose to stand, but I chose to sit at the table and twirl a glass of water in the condensation on the polished tabletop. "We were walking along, minding our own business and getting ready to stop for lunch. Mom thought someone's stomach was growling—"

"I did think it was kind of loud for that," she said, wiping the table and sliding a coaster under my glass. "But I didn't know what else it could be."

"I'll get to you, ma'am. Miss Nelson?"

"The growl came again, louder, and the bear stuck its head out of the bushes."

"Wayne threw away my whistle," Rusty pouted.

"Because you were upsetting the bear," Maryann pointed out, scowling.

I sighed. "My sister screamed, further enraging the bear. Matt and Wayne started shooting. The bear didn't go down in time and swiped at Wayne. He continued shooting and the bear died. While it was lying on the ground, we saw a knife sticking out of its shoulder. Rusty recognized the knife as one used by the chef when the guy was carving ham. Oh, and someone put a raw steak in our backpack. I presume, to attract the bear while it was wounded. That's about it."

He stared open-mouthed as the others started talking again all at once. He scratched his head, snapped his notepad closed, and marched toward the door. If I were talented as a lip-reader, I'd swear he said something about a nut house.

He stopped before going outside and said, without turning around, "I assume y'all aren't going anywhere." He left.

"Why would he say that?" Angela stared after him. "We can't possibly be suspects. Isn't that what they tell suspects?"

"I'm sure everyone at the resort is a suspect." I stood and put my hands on Cherokee's shoulders. "The decision seems to be taken away from us. Are you all right?"

"As long as I'm with all of you, I'm fine." She put a hand over mine. "I know what you'll do to keep us safe. I've seen it first hand. There's no place I'd rather be than where you are."

Okay, I was going to cry. I wrapped my arms around her from behind. "You're a strong, sweet young woman. You would have found a way to save yourself if I hadn't come up with a plan."

She tilted her head back to look up at me. "But you don't stop looking, Aunt Stormi. You're like a pit bull."

"I am, aren't I?"

Mom joined in, hugging me from behind. "That's what we Nelsons do. Go after and protect what's ours. Now, the Granger's killer has made this personal. Let's come up with one of Stormi's famous plans."

The problem with that idea is…I hadn't a clue where to go from there. "I don't know what's next." I broke up our huddle. Out of desperation, I said, "Rusty, you haven't seen or heard anything other than the bear, the hike, or the chef with the knife, have you?" I figured I should be as specific as possible.

"New chef." He stuffed a chocolate-chip cookie whole into his mouth.

"And?" I waited for him to chew and swallow.

"New knives."

"Where did the old chef go?"

"That mean woman fired him."

"Cheri?"

He nodded. "Right after ambulance take Wayne and Matt."

I couldn't imagine that the police let the man leave, though. "Do you know where the old chef is now?"

"In the bunkhouse." He shoved another cookie into his mouth, dribbling crumbs down the front of his overalls as he talked. "All the workers live in a building hidden by trees."

I suppose the resort would want something less attractive than the cottages hidden. "Can you show me?"

He nodded and shoved what was left of the cookies down the front of his bib. "Follow me."

I motioned for Maryann to come along, and did as I was told.

11

The bunkhouse, a sprawling L-shaped building painted a soft tan color, was masterfully hidden by flowering bushes and thick evergreen trees. Doors lined the long building, signifying separate living quarters. Unless you knew the dirt path led to the building, you'd have no idea. The resort clearly didn't want the guests to see such a plain, cement block building. I also had a strong guess that Cheri resided somewhere…prettier.

Rusty knocked on a door at the far end and stepped back in order for me to take over. "His name is Chef Ryan."

"Thank you."

A tall man, who looked like he was of Italian descent, answered the door. A red and black flannel shirt strained across a round belly. A thick beard covered half of his face. "Yeah? Guests aren't supposed to be back here."

"I apologize for disturbing you, but I'm a private investigator, hired by Amber Granger, to investigate her husband's death. May we come in…?"

"Ryan Bertolinni." He peered over my shoulder. "Rusty! Yes, come in."

"He's my friend," Rusty said, pushing past me.

I shot an amused glance at Maryann and stepped into a surprisingly clean room. I didn't know why I always expected men who lived alone to be messy. Obviously, it was a preconceived idea I needed to let go.

"Have a seat. I have cappuccino."

Maryann and I accepted readily. Rusty wanted a soda.

Once our host had our coffee, he sat in a large easy chair. "Well, what do you want? Isn't both of the Grangers dead?"

"Yes." I blew on my drink.

"How can you work for a dead woman?"

"Obviously, she hired me before her death." I had a feeling the man was laughing at me, but I couldn't see a smirk under all the facial hair. "You were fired for losing a knife, correct?"

"I didn't lose a knife." His eyes hardened. "I had one stolen from me. It was from a personal set. Very expensive."

"You'll get it back eventually." If he was innocent. I set my coffee on the short table in front of me, almost forgetting my resolve not to drink anything I didn't see prepared.

Maryann did the same.

Ryan laughed. "You think I'd poison you in my home? I'm already at the top of the police's suspect list. That Rodriguez said I was big enough to throw a knife at a bear. Stupid! Only a truly desperate person would do something so foolish. I am not that type of person."

"Ryan is a good cook," Rusty said. "Gives me free food. He didn't kill anyone."

"See?" Ryan's teeth flashed. "I'm innocent."

While I didn't think the man guilty, I just wasn't sure I liked him. "How could someone get their hands on one of your personal knives? Do you leave them in the kitchen?"

"Of course. Why carry them back and forth? I lock the kitchen every night. Whoever took my knife had a key card." He planted his hands on his thighs and pushed to his feet. "Now, if you'll excuse me, I've got a whole lot of nothing to do since I'm unemployed." He opened the front door. "Rusty, you come see me any time. Ladies, keep your distance. Haven't you heard? I'm mean enough to tangle with a bear." He slammed the door.

"What a rude man." Maryann stormed down the path. "We didn't learn a thing."

"We did. We learned that only someone with a key card could have taken his knife. The unfortunate thing is…we also know how easy it is to steal one." I headed for the pool area, not ready to go back to the cottage without Matt, my very own stolen key card nestled in my pocket.

My cell phone rang as I shed my shoes and stuck my aching feet into the hot tub, thankful the pool area was empty. Since it was nearing the dinner hour, the pool wouldn't be empty for long. The guests tended to gather there after they'd eaten. I pulled my phone from my pocket, relieved to see Matt's number. "Is everything okay?"

"Yes. Wayne and I are on our way back. He took ten stitches in the shoulder. Could have been worse."

I said a prayer of thanksgiving, then told Matt of my conversation with Bertolinni.

"You didn't go alone, did you?"

"No, Rusty and Maryann were with me." I left out the fact I almost drank the man's coffee. "I've learned not to investigate alone."

"That's my girl. See you in an hour. Love you." Click.

"What now?" Maryann swished her feet in the water. "We could interview someone else."

"Cheri, maybe. If anyone knows anything about everyone here, it would be her." I doubted she'd tell us anything, though. The woman took her job very seriously. "I want to get into Mr. Boyd's room." Maybe I could skip dinner and order room service. Instinct told me that Boyd Industries was not on the up and up. That sheet of fake companies and bank accounts had to be related in some way to Seth Granger quitting Boyd Industries.

"We need to find out if Seth had any family besides Amber," I said. "Maybe he told them why he quit working for Boyd." I knew I was searching for a piece of rice in a salt shaker, but I couldn't sit back and wonder. Answers didn't come to a person that way. At least not to me. I had to pound the proverbial pavement.

Voices on the other side of the hedge, signaled dinner time. "I'm going to meet Matt at the cottage, then sneak into Shelby's room. If you see her, or Lawrence, trying to leave the restaurant before I get back, stall them."

"What if they never show up at the restaurant?"

I bit my lower lip. "Pull the fire alarm. No, don't do that. Sprinklers will come on." While my books kept me supplied with a steady income, I didn't relish paying for repairs due to sprinklers. I dried my feet off with my socks, then slipped them into my shoes. "I'll think of something. If I don't see them before I head upstairs, I'll make a plan."

"Be careful. I know what your plans are like." She put on her shoes and headed for the restaurant.

I hated doing anything by the seat-of-my-pants, but there were a lot of people at this resort, and I'd made very little leeway. We'd be released as persons of interest soon and able to return home. I still had a lot to do before that happened. I never got my second massage in order to grill Bri some more, I still wanted to talk to each of the bridesmaids, and somehow, I needed to get Cheri to spill her guts. That woman had to know a ton! The trick would be getting her to talk.

Matt and Wayne weren't back yet. I glanced at my watch. I'd leave a note as to where I went and Matt could catch up with me. In the meantime, I'd take Mom. With my purse slung over my shoulder, I headed for the restaurant.

I leaned close to Mom's ear as she stood in a buffet line. "I need you to come snooping with me."

"Now?"

"Yes."

She shoved her plate into Dakota's hands and rushed after me. "This is always worth skipping dinner over."

"We'll order in later." I pressed the elevator button. "Did you see Shelby and Lawrence?"

"They didn't want the buffet. They went to the actual restaurant part."

Good. That would take longer.

Mom rubbed her hands together. "It's about time we went to their room. I was starting to think you'd lost your nerve."

"I've been kind of busy."

The elevator doors opened. Cheri stood inside, staring at the floor. She heaved a heavy sigh before noticing us waiting to get on. A heavy burden seemed to rest on her shoulders more and more each day. "Pardon me?" She brushed past us and headed in the direction of the restaurant.

I shrugged and pushed the button for the second floor. When the doors opened again, I peered out, looked both ways, then walked as fast as possible, without running, to Shelby's room. I slid the key card into the slot. "Yes! It still works."

We pushed inside. Their suite must take up most of that side of the second floor. Large windows covered one whole wall of a room designated as a living room. I peeked through the curtains.

Lara, one of the bridesmaids, ducked between a couple of the cottages. Mr. Bertolini, followed her, staying to the shadows. Behind them, trailed Cheri. What in the world was up with those three? Clouds, pregnant with rain, scudded across the moon. A flash of lightning lit up the sky.

"What are we looking for?" Mom's question pulled me back to the task at hand.

"Anything that would point to Lawrence Boyd being a crook."

"Right. I'm headed for the love nest." She opened double doors that led into a bedroom with a king-sized bed.

Spotting Lawrence's briefcase, I pulled on a pair of rubber gloves I always kept in my purse, and set the case on the table. Several files rested inside.

One contained legitimate looking pages, maybe from a slide show presentation focused on marketing. Another looked like a resume for Cheri Mason. Maybe our little manager wasn't as happy at her job as she let on. The third folder contained bank information.

I flipped through the pages. Bingo! Line after line of various large amounts of money being funneled into Boyd Industries, then into several off shore accounts. I snapped pictures with my cell phone, not forgetting Cheri's resume, then slid the folders back into the case. I froze as footsteps sounded in the hall along with raised voices. When they moved on, I exhaled deeply.

"Mom, we've got to get out of here." I stepped into the bedroom.

Mom turned from the dresser. She held a small clear bottle in her hand. The sort one might find prescription pills in. "This bottle smells like seawater." She held it up to the light. "I can't tell if that little blob use to be a jellyfish or not."

"Bring it with us. We should go." I took a quick glance around, fully intending to pay another visit to the room. But, experience had taught me that staying too long only resulted in disaster.

I hurried and opened the door, letting out a shriek to see someone standing there. When I got over my shock, I smacked Matt in the chest. "You scared me to death! What are you doing out here?"

"Keeping guard. You closed the door, so I couldn't get in." He gave me the crooked smile that always sent my heart flying. "Let's go back to the cottage and share information."

"You found out something? When?" We strolled back to the elevator.

"I made a few calls while Wayne was getting stitched up. I thought it prudent to look into Seth's background."

"I was thinking the same thing."

The three of us got into the elevator. Matt pressed the button for the first floor.

The elevator lowered, then stopped with a jerk. We stood in silence for several seconds before the elevator started to move again. Upwards this time, then down again, only to stop with a jerk. By the third time, my stomach roiled.

"What in the heck?" I braced my hands on the walls.

Mom pressed the call button with urgent frequency. "Why isn't anyone answering? I'm going to throw up from all this bouncing."

The light flickered out, casting us into complete darkness.

"What happened?" My heart hammered in my ears.

"I think we lost electricity. It was getting ready to storm when I came into the building."

I could hear him moving around. "Check the panels overhead."

"That only happens in the movies, sweetheart."

Oh. "Then what are you looking for?"

"Something that opens the door."

"I'm pressing all of the buttons," Mom said. "Nothing is happening. If we start jerking again—Oh!"

The elevator sank like an amusement park ride. We stopped with a jolt and the doors opened onto complete darkness. I had a flashlight app on my cell phone, and pressed the button to give us some light. "I didn't know this place had a basement." None of the buttons showed that it did.

"Let me see your phone." Matt held it up. "Smell that?"

"What?"

"Tobacco." He pointed to what looked like a large amount of dried herbs, a bucket of water, and some cheesecloths. "I'm willing to guess someone else is about to be poisoned."

12

"How?" I glanced up at Matt.

"You soak the tobacco leaves, then drain through a cheesecloth, making the strongest liquid nicotine possible. Very toxic." He wrapped the evidence in the cheesecloth. "Let's get out of here before your phone battery dies."

Too late. The light continued to dim until it cast us into total darkness again before we reached the elevator. "Matt?"

"Stretch out your hand until you touch me. Grab a hold of my belt loop. Anne, you do the same. I saw some stairs to our right. I'll try to find them."

"I have a cigarette lighter in my purse," Mom said.

"Why? You don't smoke," I said.

"For emergencies. I used to carry a screwdriver as a weapon until I bought my gun. I wasn't keen on the idea of hand-to-hand combat. Here it is!" Soon, a small flame lit up a one-foot area around us. "I thought I taught you girls to be prepared for anything."

"This will do." Matt handed me the confiscated evidence, then took the lighter from Mom. He held it high, hissing occasionally when the flame got too close to his fingers.

A door slammed. A lock clicked into place. So much for locating the stairs.

"Someone just locked us in." Fear spread through me like a forest fire. I didn't like the dark, wasn't exactly afraid of it, but that little flame from the lighter wouldn't last forever.

"Stay close," Matt said. "I'm here. You aren't alone."

"God is with us," Mom added.

I think Matt meant himself, but knowing both, three counting Mom, were in the dark with me was a huge comfort. "Any ideas?"

"It's a basement. Most of them have at least a small window." He let the flame die. "I'll light it again in a second. It's burning my fingers."

I nodded, knowing he couldn't see me, and not caring. I stood so close to him, I could feel his body heat. He radiated a lot of heat. But enough to smoke? Wait. I sniffed. "Is that smoke?" My heart stopped.

"It is. Let's find that window fast." He lit the flame again. "There."

I caught a glimpse of shiny glass when lightning streaked. "There's something in front of the window."

"Just boxes, I think. Anne, hold the lighter."

Mom held it close to her face, her eyes wide. "This would make a great horror flick. Three people trapped in a basement, smoke filling the room, and a psycho in the corner with an ax. All we're missing is the psycho."

That was debatable. "Please, be quiet." This was not the time for her imagination to convince mine to join her scary fantasies.

"Just trying to break the silence. That's what scares me the most. Silence."

Matt stepped away. Thuds of boxes being tossed filled the space.

"Maybe we should call the fire department," Mom said.

"That would be nice if we had a phone. Mine is dead." Seriously?

"I have mine."

Silence screamed in a basement quickly filling with

smoke. My eyes watered.

"Why didn't you say something before?" Uh-oh. Matt had lost his patience.

"We were looking for a light," Mom said. "I don't have the flashlight app on my phone. I'm a bit stressed, and obviously not thinking clearly."

"It still provides *light*." He said the last word sharply. "Call Wayne, then call the fire department. In that order. Now."

"Okay, no need to get mean." The face of Mom's phone lit up. "Wayne? It's Anne. Matt, Stormi, and I are trapped in a basement under the main building. It's filling with smoke. I need you to find us, quickly, please. Matt is losing his patience. I have to call the fire department now. Bye!"

"What did he say?" I asked.

"I got his voice mail."

For crying out loud! Was nothing going to go right? "Then, call someone else! Dakota or Maryann."

"I will as soon as…Yes? 911? Thank you, Jesus. We're trapped in a basement that's on fire at the Mountain Springs Resort. At least, I think it's on fire. I fear we'll probably be dead by the time you get here, but I was told to make the call…I'm sorry. I can't stay on the line. I have other calls to make. Hurry, please." She sighed. "I can feel you rolling your eyes, Stormi, but you know I'm right. It will take the fire department at least twenty minutes to get here, and I can feel the smoke tickling my throat. I'll be coughing next, then dying of smoke inhalation."

"You're just the bearer of grave news, aren't you?" I clutched the evidence to my chest in a vain effort to gain some comfort.

"Hold that thought. My phone is ringing. It's Wayne." Mom repeated her message. "Okay, he's coming."

Tears rolled down my face. Tears I chose to chalk up to

the smoke rather than the fact I'd almost lost hope. "Matt?"

"I'm here. Trying to find something to break the window."

I thought my eyes had adjusted to the dark, but realized now that a weak light shined from where Matt stood. A face appeared at the window. Mom gasped.

I'd never been so happy to see Rusty in my life. Seconds later, the glass shattered, and welcome air rushed in.

"Window is too small," Rusty said.

"Even for me?" I moved forward quickly, taking deep breaths.

"Yep. Wayne is looking for door." He disappeared.

Matt placed his good arm around me. "See? Nothing to worry about."

"Except for the fact that no matter what I do, someone will try to kill me."

"Well, we were snooping."

"Thanks for pointing that out." I rested my cheek against his chest that rumbled with laughter. "Does this mean that Shelby is our killer?"

"It does raise her and Boyd to the top of the list."

Light from an industrial flashlight flooded the room. "Y'all ready to come out?" Wayne's voice was the sweetest thing I'd heard in a good long while. "There was no fire, just a smoking pile of rags."

A warning, perhaps? Did this mean we were getting close to finding the culprit? I wanted to confront Shelby in the worst way. If she was the one to lock us down here, I wanted to punch her in the throat. Not that I would, unless she came at me, but I'd let the desire simmer for a few minutes, then stomp it down with reason and the threat of jail.

By the time we stepped outside, the rain had stopped, a fire truck was roaring onto the property, and a crowd had gathered. Their reflections shimmered in rain puddles. I couldn't help but think how much like a murder mystery scene the night portrayed.

I shoved the evidence into Matt's arms and allowed a hunky fireman to strap an oxygen mask to my nose and mouth. Oh, the sweet oxygen.

Other firemen rushed to check the building for safety. Guests milled around, staring at me, Mom, and Matt as if we were exotic creatures in a tank.

Angela marched toward me, a murderous look on her face. She grabbed my mask, pulled it away from my face, and released it. It snapped against my skin with a stinging whap.

"Ow! What was that for?" I moved the mask, more tenderly than she had.

She crossed her arms. "We may fight. A lot. But, I do love you. Would you please stop standing at death's door, knocking to get in?"

"You were worried?" A warmth rose in my heart, chasing away the chill from an evening soaked with rain.

"You had Mom with you. Of course I was worried." She tossed her hair over her shoulder and flounced away, leaving me with a grin on my face and feeling loved.

Officer Rodriguez stormed by and gave me a stern glance. He probably thought I was somehow responsible for the night's events. Maybe I was. I removed my oxygen mask and followed him. If I stayed on the outskirts of the crowd, maybe I could eavesdrop while he questioned other people.

He approached Cheri first, probably because she was the resort manager. He stepped to a patio table and motioned for her to sit. Perfect. A nearby bush gave me a wonderful vantage point.

"I promise you, Officer Rodriguez," Cheri said, folding her hands in her lap. "I have no idea how the door to the basement got locked. Guests are not allowed down there. We use it strictly for storage."

"What about the paraphernalia for making concentrated nicotine?" His pencil poised over his pad.

"Another mystery." She tilted her head. "Am I a suspect?"

"Everyone, other than the three in the basement, and Detective Jones, are persons of interest. That includes you, Miss Mason."

"I never should have allowed that Nelson woman and her group to rent a cottage from me. It's not as if everyone in the state of Arkansas hasn't heard how trouble follows her." Cheri exhaled heavily, then stood. "Are we finished here? I have things to tend to."

"For now." After she left, he parted the bush. "You can come out now."

"How did you know I was there?"

You reek of smoke." He glanced to where Cheri approached an older couple. "So did she." A muscle ticked in his jaw.

"Any reason why she would?"

"Well, she did go to the basement to see things for herself, she says." He slid his notepad into his pocket. "Try not to get killed on my watch, Miss Nelson." He strolled away as if his words were nothing more than casual conversation.

Cheri and Shelby took turns being my primary suspect. I made a mental note to interview each of them very soon.

Rodriguez approached a group of resort employees next. I didn't bother to hide this time. Instead, I fished my private investigator's badge from my purse and clipped it to my waistband. If I were lucky, the employees would think I was a legitimate person in the investigation, instead of a recently cleared person of interest.

Officer Rodriguez wrote down names, even Bertolinni's,

who hung on the outskirts. I swerved and stood in front of the ex-chef.

"You were spotted disappearing with one of the guests a while ago. Mind telling me where you were going?" I put on my sternest face, which I'd been told wasn't very stern. Still, it was all I had.

"Can't a man meet a pretty lady for a little rendezvous without getting the third degree?" His eyes practically disappeared under the weight of his eyebrows as they drew together in a scowl.

I shrugged. "You were followed by Cheri Mason. Were you aware of that fact?"

He said a word I couldn't repeat, then ran both hands through his thick hair. "That woman has her nose in everyone else's business. I no longer work here. Remind her that she fired me and that my life is now private."

"Was it not private before?"

"Not even a little bit. She has a curfew for the workers, we can't fraternize with each other, and we have to let her know days in advance if we're leaving the resort for any reason. She takes her job a little too seriously. If it weren't for the murder investigation, I'd have been sent packing ten minutes after getting fired. It's all about the money to her." He leaned closer. "I've often suspected that she pinches pennies this hard so she can divert some to her personal account."

I followed his gaze over my shoulder.

Cheri glared at us from twenty feet away.

13

After a sleepless night dreaming of bear attacks and dark basements, I sat by the silent pool and nursed a cup of coffee. It might not be the same frozen blend I got from my friend, Norma, but it was cold, mocha flavored, and full of caffeine.

In less than a week, if the local authorities allowed, my family and I would head home where it was relatively safe. I'd leave that instant if my niece and nephew weren't so set on cramming the remaining days full of fun. Ziplining, horseback riding, and other activities to show me just how out of shape I'd become. Still, our vacation had been anything but. We deserved some fun before heading home.

The trick would be staying alive that long.

"Hey, beautiful." Matt lowered himself into a lounge chair next to me. "Sleep okay?"

I shook my head. "Too much garbage up here." I tapped my head.

"We could question some people and, either add or detract, from all those thoughts." He smiled, sending my heart fluttering. I prayed he would always have the effect of making me lose coherent thought with one glance into his amazing eyes.

"We could talk about it over breakfast."

A dimple appeared in his right cheek. "Do you mind if we choose a table to ourselves?"

"You read my mind." I stood, holding out my hand to help him to his feet. "We've had very little alone time since you arrived." At home, we spent many hours cuddled together on the sofa, pretending to watch television.

If I was involved in a mystery, we didn't go out much. A simple dinner at a restaurant had proven to be too hazardous. Not to mention the restaurant managers asked us not to come back. After several busted windows and bullet holes, they feared their insurance rates would escalate too high for them to pay. Not to mention the many times Matt went away for undercover work. Needless to say, when we had the opportunity for alone time, we took it.

"What about ordering in?" I asked.

"I'd love that, but going to the dining room allows us to scope out who we want to interview."

I linked my arm with his. "You're so smart." I grinned up at him. "That's why I love you."

"The only reason?"

"Nah, your kisses are pretty spectacular."

After he took a few minutes to prove just how wonderful his kisses were, we headed to breakfast. I spotted the group of bridesmaids right away, minus Shelby, of course. I doubted Lawrence would allow her out of his sight anytime soon.

"I want to ask Lara, the blond, a few questions," I said, as I sat across from Matt. I explained to him about seeing her, the former chef, and Cheri while I'd snooped in Shelby's suite.

"Sounds good. Anyone else?"

I scanned the room. "It wouldn't hurt to ask the maids a few questions. They usually see much more than they let on."

"Rodriguez questioned them."

"But, they might talk to me easier than they would him."

"Agreed." He winked. "That's why I love you. You're so smart."

I laughed and grabbed our plates. "You sit and I'll get our breakfast. It's easier for me to carry these than it is you with one arm. I'll get you some of everything." Including slices of ham the new chef was carving. He didn't look old enough to be out of culinary school.

I waited until the line dissipated and stepped up to the counter. "Two slices of ham on this plate, and one on this plate, please." I flashed a grin. "You're new…" I peered at his name tag. "Evan. How do you like it here?"

He glanced over my shoulder. "It's good."

"Wonderful. Are the other workers kind to you?" I followed his gaze to see Cheri staring in our direction. "The last chef was well-liked."

He shrugged.

I leaned closer. "I've also heard Cheri is a tyrant."

He paled. "She isn't so bad."

"Miss Nelson, I hope everything is to your liking?" Cheri said from behind me.

"Wonderful." I turned. "Just welcoming Evan."

Her smile didn't reach her eyes. "Thank you for being so kind, but he really does have a lot of work to do."

"I apologize." I took my plates to the buffet, adding Evan to the list of people I wanted to speak with.

When I returned to our table, I wasn't thrilled to see Rusty scarfing down a plate of scrambled eggs and hashbrowns. I raised my eyebrows at Matt as I handed him his plate.

"Sorry." He shrugged.

I understood. None of us wanted to hurt Rusty's feelings by telling him to eat somewhere else, but not only had I wanted to be alone with Matt, but the other man's table manners left a lot to be desired.

He chewed with his mouth open, dropping crumbs down the front of him, and shoveled food into his mouth like a bulldozer, even going so far as to lift his plate to bring it closer to his mouth. I shuddered and looked away.

"Add the new chef to our list," I said.

Rusty glanced up. "He's Cheri's nephew." He went back to eating.

Interesting. "How do you know this?"

"He said."

Alrighty, then. "Rusty, do you know which maid cleans the Boyds' suite?"

"Susan."

Maybe I should make Rusty a partner in my private investigation business. He had more information than an encyclopedia. I had no idea how he did it.

"She is afraid of Cheri." Rusty brushed off the front of his overalls, bounded from his seat, and then dashed back to the buffet.

Matt chuckled. "He loves that the food is free. I bet he has a week's worth stashed under his bed. Dakota has been complaining about a bad smell."

I made a mental note to increase his salary as my gardener. "We have Evan, Amy, and Lara to speak to. That's a good start to the day."

"Snooping without me?" Mom crossed her arms.

A stern Maryann stood next to her. "Or me?"

"We can't all go." I frowned. "It'll be like an interrogation." I knew Matt and I should have eaten in the cottage.

"Why don't the two of you get another massage," Matt offered. "See if you can get more information out of Bri. That way, we'll finish faster."

"At least someone appreciates our talents." Mom huffed and stomped away, Matt's sister on her heels.

"Clever man. I did want to talk to Bri again."

"If you don't give your mother work to do, she'll create her own. We both know that doesn't always turn out well."

True. We finished breakfast, stacked our dishes on the counter provided for dirty dishes, then stepped out into bright sunshine. It promised to be a glorious day.

"Let's find the maid, Susan," I suggested. "Evan won't be off duty for an hour or two, and Lara is still in the dining room."

"Hold my hand. We'll pretend to take a stroll. When we find her, we'll ask some questions. I hope you have a plan to get her to talk."

"I'm working on one." I entwined my fingers with his. "What are we going to do with the papers I found in Shelby's suitcase?"

"I'm still waiting to see how much money are in the accounts, the names of the fake businesses, and the best way of proving Lawrence Boyd is a fraud." He sighed. "I'm sure it will mean the Feds taking over."

"Worth it if it gets a killer off the street."

"Very true." He squeezed my hand. "Just make sure no one knows you have a copy of those papers. I have a feeling someone other than Boyd is looking for them."

"You're pretty sure he isn't the killer."

"Yes. He's dirty, but I don't think he killed Seth or his wife."

"Shelby?"

"I'm not sure about her. She strikes me as the type to do anything to keep her lifestyle the way she wants it."

I spotted an older woman in a traditional black and white maid's uniform stepping out of one of the cottages. "Susan?"

She stopped and looked our way, confirming that she was, indeed, the maid we looked for. "May I help you?" She lifted some towels from her cart. "Clean towels?"

"No, thank you." I pulled my ID badge from my pocket. "We'd like to ask you a few questions."

Her friendly expression turned impassive. "I've told the police all I know."

"Please. I was hired by Mrs. Granger to find out who killed her husband. Now, she's dead, too. Don't you think they deserve justice?"

She sighed. "What cottage are you in?"

I told her.

"I'll be there in five minutes. I'll answer while I clean, but no longer than that."

"Thank you." I tugged Matt after me. "See? She'll talk."

"Maybe. What are you going to do if she doesn't show?"

"Hunt her down." I unlocked the door to my cottage, relieved no one was there, then quickly made a paper sign telling everyone other than housekeeping to stay out and taped it to the outside of the door. Hopefully, my family would take the hint and stay out.

Five minutes later, seven if you wanted to be exact, Susan let herself in. She headed straight for the bathroom my mother used. "If you want to talk, you must follow me. I'll be fired if I don't do my job by ten."

I glanced at Matt, then motioned for him to stay in the living room. I followed Susan, and leaned against the doorframe of the bathroom. "Do you like working here?"

"It pays the bills and gives me a free place to live." She rolled clean towels and stuck them in alcoves under the sink. "I don't think that's the question you want to ask, now is it?" She straightened. "You want to know whether I know anything about the Grangers' deaths."

"Yes." Okay, no pretense. This woman was a straight-shooter. "If you tell me what you know, we won't waste any time."

"I don't know who killed them," she said, wiping the

counter. "But, I did overhear Mr. Lawrence telling his slutty girlfriend that she had gone overboard this time. I also heard him say that Shelby was the reason Seth found the information and quit." She moved to the toilet. "I don't know what information he was talking about. Once he discovered me standing in the hall, he slammed the door closed." She grinned. "He had left it open a bit. In a big hurry to get that woman alone."

So far, I wasn't learning anything new. We knew Boyd had information he didn't want known, we suspected Seth had known something about it, and we knew Shelby was as dirty as the bottom of a sewer worker's shoe. "Did you ever hear the Grangers talking about anything suspicious?"

"I found this in the tub." She pulled a vial, similar to the one Mom had found in Shelby's room, from her apron pocket. "This is why I was late coming to your room. I had to go get it." She held it up. "I was careful not to touch the murderous little bugger."

"You know what this is?" My stomach sank. Had I just found another suspect?

"Of course. I heard the police talking. This, my dear, is what killed Seth Granger. I found it caught in hairs in the tub drain. Don't worry, it's dead."

She turned the vial in the light from the bathroom window.

Floating in a tiny bit of water was a jellyfish no bigger than my fingernail.

"Want to know the best part?" She grinned.

I nodded, holding my breath.

"I also found one of these buggers in the drain of the Boyd suite."

14

When Susan left our cottage, I handed the vial to Matt. He turned it this way and that in the light.

"Weird that such a little thing can be so deadly. Might have been a beauty before it shriveled up. How in the world did she spot something so tiny?"

"She said she was cleaning the drain. She must be very meticulous." Looking for items of value, would be my guess.

He slid the vial into his pocket. "Maybe I'm wrong about Lawrence Boyd. This sure makes him look suspicious."

"Unless someone is setting him up." I plopped onto the sofa. "Maybe we need to go over the airline manifests again. Someone other than the Grangers went to Australia."

"Yeah, the girlfriend." He sat next to me and propped his feet on the glass-topped coffee table. "We just need to figure out her name."

"It's someone here at the resort. We're too remote for an unknown person to come on the grounds, kill the Grangers, lock us in the basement, all without being seen." I chewed my cuticle, staring through the open curtains. "Maybe we need to look at other names. An alias, a middle name, anything but what we're looking at now."

"Come on." He grabbed my hand and pulled me to my feet. "Maybe you'll see something I missed."

He led me to his cottage. When we stepped inside, my

sister and Wayne bolted to sitting positions from the couch.

I grinned. "Did we interrupt something?"

"Yes." Wayne glowered. "I thought you two were investigating."

"We are." Matt pulled a briefcase from under the sofa and withdrew several sheets of papers. "We need to go over these again." He explained what the maid had found.

Wayne sighed and reached for the papers. "Give me a few."

Angela rolled her eyes and pouted. "I guess I'll go for my facial." She grabbed her purse and stormed out.

For several minutes, the only sound was the rustling of paper. I scanned the list of names, searching for anything that didn't seem to fit. Nothing jumped out at me. "This is a waste of time. Unless the alias, if there is one, is close to the real name, we won't find it." I tossed the three sheets I had onto the coffee table. "We don't even know if there is an alias."

"It's easy enough to get a fake ID nowadays." Matt's papers joined mine. "Let's go talk to a few more people. Maybe we'll get lucky again. Wayne, try finding out who the Marshal was on the flight Seth Granger took. Maybe he noticed something out of the ordinary, or a description of the woman he was with."

"It's a long shot." Wayne leaned forward and opened a laptop. "See y'all later. You might want to pray for a miracle."

He was correct. I'd prayed for safety, but not for guidance or wisdom. I needed to slow down and listen. Maybe God had been giving me a nudge that I'd ignored. I stopped on the pathway to Matt's cottage.

"What are you doing?" Matt cocked his head.

"Waiting for a nudge."

After several seconds, Evan, the new chef walked by,

slapping his chef hat against his leg and muttering words I couldn't repeat. I smiled and thanked God for the nudge. If Evan was angry with someone, he might be more willing to talk.

We followed him to the entrance to the path that led to the workers' housing. "Evan!"

He turned, frowning when he saw me. "Haven't you gotten me into enough trouble?"

"What do you mean?"

"I was informed by my dear aunt that fraternizing with the guests is prohibited. I guess speaking with you while carving your meat counts as that."

"You aren't working now."

He sighed. "What do you want?"

I glanced at Matt who gave me the go-ahead to ask the questions. "I know you're new here, but you're bound to have heard about the murders."

"Yeah. So?" He crossed his arms and leaned against a fence post.

"Would you mind sharing what you've heard? I know the workers talk about the guests." I flashed my ID badge. "I was hired by one of the victims, and now that she's gone, I still feel compelled to solve her death."

He glanced around. "Let's just say this isn't the sweet resort it looks like. There is a seedy underground that rivals anything you'll find in the big city. Sex, drugs, you name it, we have it."

"Anyone going by a false name?"

He paled. "Why would you ask that?"

"Who is it, Evan?"

"I gotta go. You're on the right track. Keep sniffing." He whirled and dashed away.

"We're getting close, Matt."

He put his arm around my shoulder. "Let's find that

bridesmaid. If Shelby was having a fling with Seth, maybe she kissed and told."

We could hope.

After a few moments of searching, I found her in the sauna. I wasn't dressed for a steam bath, but I kicked off my shoes and entered the room anyway.

I couldn't see or breathe. The tiny room was so full of steam and eucalyptus, it was like stepping into a hot, muggy, cloud that stung my sinuses.

"You're supposed to be naked," Lara said from somewhere in the corner. "Or at least wrapped in a towel."

"No time. I got the urge." I made my way to the bench, stubbing my toe in the process. Talking was going to be difficult. Already, the steam left a bad taste in my mouth. This was not an experience I'd do again anytime soon.

"Breathe through your nose."

I couldn't talk that way.

"And make sure you lift your legs when you hear the spray release."

"Why?"

A jet of boiling air hit my calves. Ow! I drew my knees up to my chest. "Is this supposed to be relaxing?"

"It's good for your skin."

This had to be what hell was like. All we were missing was the smell of sulphur.

"Mind answering a few questions?"

"I've got ten minutes. Spill."

"Has Shelby made a trip to Australia within the last couple of months?"

"Not that I know of. She would have definitely bragged about it."

"How long had she been seeing Seth Granger?"

"Over a year. Then, he quit Boyd Industries, and she turned her attention to bigger fish." Her hand clamped my arm. "You need to stop asking questions. That's how people die."

I felt like I was already dying.

"There was a week that nobody could get a hold of her," Lara said. "Maybe she was in Australia. I don't think she killed Seth, though. She doesn't like to lose her toys, living or otherwise. Seth Granger was a player. He probably had more than one girl in the wings. I'm telling you, Shelby isn't a killer. A slut, yes."

The steam released again. I couldn't take it anymore. "Would she have gone by another name?"

"Mason Lereux. She's from French descent somewhere down the line and likes to play pretend."

I caught a glimpse of her rising from the steam like a drenched goddess. I averted my eyes from her nudeness. "Thank you."

"Don't tell anyone I told you anything. I'm not ready to die." She stepped out of the sauna and left me to follow.

Cold air slapped me in the face. I shivered and grabbed a towel, wrapping it around me before joining Matt.

"You're insane." He rubbed my arms. "Let's get you into some dry clothes."

As we walked, I filled him in on my conversation with Lara. "I saw that name on the manifest. What do you bet Mason is in the seat next to Seth?"

"Why is everyone so certain Shelby *isn't* the killer?" Matt opened the door to my cottage. "All signs point to her."

"Too convenient?"

"Maybe. If we find a Mason on that flight, we'll go ask Shelby a few more questions."

I headed for my bedroom as Matt shouted out, "Bingo!"

After a quick shower, I dressed in a clean pair of jeans, a purple and black flannel shirt, and tied my hair back into a ponytail. I stepped back into the living room to see Matt and

Wayne bent over a notepad filled with names.

Matt tapped the pad with a pencil. "Here are all the females on that flight. Several of them are within a row or two of Seth Granger. Wayne spoke to the Marshal, who confirmed a woman of Shelby's description was hanging all over our victim. Another woman, dark hair, and wearing sunglasses she never removed, seemed very interested in the couple. The Marshal said her hair was definitely a wig, and a cheap one, at that."

"That could be anyone. Amber?"

"No. Remember, we found her on a later flight."

Right. "So, now what?"

"We question Shelby. This time, I do the talking." Matt pulled his badge from his pocket and clipped it to his belt. "Wayne, feel like coming along?"

"You bet."

I wasn't about to be left behind. I followed them to the main building, hoping we could speak with Shelby without her watchdog fiancé. Not wanting a repeat of getting stuck in the elevator, we took the stairs.

Matt opened the door at the top, then closed it and stepped back. "Just a second. Lawrence is leaving. We won't have much time to question Shelby. He doesn't stay gone long."

"How do you know this?"

"Rusty." He grinned.

Of course. Our own personal Peeping Tom, uh, spy.

I counted to ten before Matt opened the door again. I stayed behind the men, more than happy to let them put on their "detective faces".

Matt knocked on the door. When no one answered, he knocked again, louder and harder.

"Geez. Give me a second." Shelby, wrapped in a fluffy white towel, answered the door. Her irritation turned to flirtation upon spotting the men. "Why, hello?"

"May we come in, Miss Richards." Matt glanced at me with a look on his face that said, "Get me out of here". I felt the same way when I caught a glimpse of Shelby.

"Sure." She stepped back, her towel slipping a bit. "I'm not decent, but I don't mind if you don't."

I rolled my eyes and followed the men into an apartment strewn with designer clothes. Didn't the woman ever clean up after herself?

"Don't mind the mess. I just got back from the boutique." She plopped on the sofa, the slit in the towel exposing a mile of bare thigh.

I wanted to grab something to throw over her. To their credit, the stern expression on Matt and Wayne never slipped. They'd probably seen worse in their line of work. I put on my own impassive face and kept my face averted from toned, tanned thighs.

"We know that you went to Australia with Seth Granger under the name Mason Lereux," Matt said. "Mind telling us why you lied?"

"Can't you figure that out for yourself? Lawrence would have killed me." She studied her manicure. "Besides, that's all spilt…milk at this point."

She had to be the most heartless person I'd ever met. "Did you recognize anyone else from the resort on that flight?" I asked.

"I only had eyes for Seth. Besides, could anyone who works here be able to afford a trip like that?"

I made a disgusted noise and turned away. My cell phone vibrated in my pocket. I checked the incoming text. Mom.

Come to the sauna. Now.

I showed it to Matt.

He nodded. "Miss Mason, I don't need to tell you not to go anywhere, do I?"

She shook her head. "Lawrence will not be pleased."

"I don't give a fig what Lawrence wants." Matt took my arm and led me from the room. "Call your mother."

I nodded, as we passed a stony-faced Mr. Boyd. No, the man would not be pleased. I pressed the number three on my cell phone.

"What's up, Mom?"

"We have a body in the sauna."

15

"**W**ho is it?" I reached around Mom and turned off the steam. Threaded through the door handle was the sash to a white robe.

"I've never seen her before. I noticed the sash and peered through the steam. It wasn't easy, but you can tell there's a person lying on the bench."

Matt unwound the sash and yanked open the door. He rushed inside. "It's Susan."

"Is she dead?" I asked, my heart sinking.

"Not yet. Call an ambulance." He exited the sauna with a limp Susan in his arms. He laid her on a nearby padded bench. "Get me some cool cloths."

While Mom dialed 911, I grabbed the nearest towel and soaked it in the sink. No more questioning guests or workers. I couldn't handle a death on my conscience because I got nosy. We'd been cleared to go home, but wanting justice for my client kept me here, risking the lives of everyone I loved. I was a misguided fool.

I handed Matt the towel and plopped on a different bench than the one he'd draped Susan over. My father's unsolved murder drove me to find justice for others. The single-minded determination was going to get me, or another family member, killed. I needed help. Mental help.

"What's wrong?" Mom sat next to me and peered into

my face.

"I have to stop doing this." I blinked back tears. "I can't solve Dad's murder, so I feel compelled to put myself, and you, in danger. It has to stop. I'm a writer, not a detective."

She put her arm around me and pulled me close. "You're a wonderful writer and a good investigator. Your kind heart drudges up these feelings you fight against. Let them come. Remember the good you've done over the last year."

"I keep putting everyone I love in danger." The tears spilled over. "How long until someone I love dies?"

"We help you because we want to. Look, sweetie." She tilted my face to hers and wiped my tears away with her fingers. "I'm fifty years old. Other than the years I was married to your father, I'm having the time of my life. If God calls me home at the hands of a madman, then so be it. If I didn't want to be here, I wouldn't be."

"But Angela—"

"Pshaw. She grumbles, but the excitement gives her something to talk about at work." Mom leaned back on her hands. "You keep doing good where you can."

"I should let the police handle things and throw my PI badge in the trash."

"The police can't do everything. If they could, we would have justice for your father."

I would have to do some heavy praying about whether I wanted to keep doing investigative work in the name of research for my novels. I was a best-selling author before true crime romantic mysteries, I would be so without them.

Cheri, accompanied by Rodriguez and two paramedics, rushed into the sauna.

Rodriguez took one look at me and shook his head. "If you weren't with Steele, I'd think you were the perp."

"I have a knack for being in the wrong place at the wrong time."

Cheri patted Susan's face. "Sweetie? Open your eyes. It's me. You're going to be just fine."

"Excuse me." A paramedic shouldered her out of the way.

"She's my employee." Cheri planted her fists on her hips.

"You're in our way and preventing us from caring for her. She could die, ma'am."

Cheri exhaled sharply and stepped back. I couldn't help but feel that she wasn't as worried as she let on. If I'd ever met an ice queen, she was it, except for the one moment of vulnerability when I'd caught her crying next to the pool, the woman was as heartless as a shark.

She picked up the robe's sash. "This belongs to Shelby Mason."

"How do you know?" I stood.

"See the pink ribbon along the edge? I've seen her wear it plenty of times." She tossed the sash at Rodriguez. "Are you going to solve these problems or will I have to take matters into my own hands?"

"Please, don't do that, Miss Mason. We already have our hands full with Miss Nelson."

"Hey! I'm helping." He soon had not only me glaring at him, but Cheri, too.

"How are you helping?" He narrowed his eyes. "You leave a path of destruction wherever you go."

"That's enough." Matt stepped between us. "She's found out plenty. Which I will fill you in on in private." He leaned close to me. "I'll see you back at the cottage when I'm finished here."

I nodded and motioned for Mom to follow. Instead of heading back to my cottage, I headed for the workers' quarters. The one place we'd never snooped in was Cheri's room. I needed to find out where she stayed and figure out how to get in.

"Where are we going?" Mom asked, hitching her purse high on her shoulder.

"To find Rusty." If I wanted to know anything about anyone, he was always the one to ask. "He's probably hanging out with the chef."

"No, I'm not." Rusty parted the bushes next to us.

I screamed and jumped. "How many times do I have to ask you not to leap out at me?"

"I heard my name." He stepped onto the path. "What can I say?"

I wasn't sure if he was actually asking me what I wanted to know, or alluding to the fact he was being himself and wanted to know what question to answer. "Where does Cheri live?"

He shuddered. "You don't want to go there."

"Yes, I do."

He shook his head. "She's a bad woman."

"I understand that, but this is important."

He stood his ground. "You tell Rusty what to look for. I will do it."

I groaned. He was impossible. "I can't explain it to you. It's something I'll know if I see it."

"Let me." Mom took on 'that' look that mothers are famous for. "Listen here, young man. I am giving you a direct order. Tell us where Cheri lives or you do not get dessert tonight. Understand? We will put you on the next bus home. Alone."

His eyes widened and he nodded. "Second floor. Room thirteen." He whirled and raced away.

Mom clapped her hands. "That, my dear, is how it is done."

"You're amazing." I linked my arm with hers and headed for the heavy doors that provided entrance into the dormitory-like building.

"I'm telling you she killed Susan! I saw it with my own eyes."

I froze, then peered around the corner to see Bri conversing with Chef Bertolinni. Was it possible I was actually in the right place at the right time for once?

"You actually saw her put a sash around the handle?" He crossed his massive arms. "Pretty risky, isn't it?"

Bri ducked her head. "I saw her coming from the sauna just minutes before I went in. When I saw the sash, I ran straight here. There's no way I'm getting involved."

"Who?" Mom whispered.

I shushed her, trying to figure that tidbit out for myself.

"That bridal party is bad news," Bertolinni said. "One of them played me like a fiddle, then laughed in my face when I tried to play nice. Someone needs to solve these murders so we can all get out of here. I need to find new employment."

"That writer is trying to find the killer. Maybe we should help her."

"No." He shook her. "We can't lose anyone else. We shouldn't even be talking about it." He glanced around. "There are ears everywhere."

"You're paranoid." She jerked free. "Until the deaths of that couple, nothing bad ever happened here."

"That has changed, hasn't it? We're working in a death trap."

"What do you know?"

He shook his head. "If I tell you, you'll be in danger. I've said too much. Go to your room and stay there until your shift."

I gripped Mom's hand. "We have to talk to him before he disappears."

Bri dashed up a set of stairs to her right, leaving the big man alone in a room that looked a step above a fraternity house. I cleared my throat and stepped around the corner.

"You again?" He groaned and fell into a chair, the wood creaking under him. "I suppose you heard?"

"Yep, sorry. We actually were here to talk to someone else, but you'll do."

"We can't talk here. Meet me in the woods in half an hour."

"No way," Mom said. "You could shoot us in the head and leave us for the bears."

His eyes widened. "I wouldn't do that."

She shrugged.

"There has to be somewhere else…private, but where we could call for help if you try anything." I glanced out the window. "The garden?"

"Ears out there, too." He sighed. "Meet me down the hill that leads to this place. Only go as far as you feel comfortable. Bring your man if it makes you feel safer."

"Okay," I said, leading Mom from the building.

"He isn't going to show," she said.

"Probably not, but we can't make him. If he doesn't show up, we'll have Rodriguez interrogate him."

"There is something about that man that doesn't ring true."

"Which one?" I turned to stare at her.

"Rodriguez. If he was an officer worth his salt, he should have found out something. Any information dug up has come from us."

I bit my lower lip. Mom was right. Unless the cop kept things close to his vest, he hadn't discovered any information to solve the murders. Now, why was that? If he'd heard about the offshore accounts, he could have turned dirty. Cops did it all the time when money was involved. I needed to talk to Matt asap, and now, I'd gone and made an appointment that would most likely result in nothing more than a waste of time.

After finding out that Matt and Wayne were still with Rodriguez, Mom and I headed down the road to where we could see the resort if we stood on our tiptoes. Fifteen minutes passed, then ten. Bertolinni wasn't coming.

"There he is." Mom pointed to the rise of the hill. "He's running."

The big man raced as if the hounds of hell were on his heels. From the wild waving of his hands, I gathered we should scatter. I dashed into the bushes on one side of the road, Mom the other. Seconds later, Mr. Bertolinni joined me.

"Keep going," he said.

"Is this a ploy to separate me from help?"

"It's to keep you alive." He shoved me to the ground. "I swear someone took a shot at me when I came out of the dormitory."

My heart skipped a beat. "Are you sure?"

"Pretty sure. I heard a pop, then rocks peppered my feet. What else could it have been?"

Maybe Bri was right and the man *was* paranoid. "It doesn't appear as if anyone is chasing you now. They would have had a clear shot of you running down the middle of the road."

"You think I'm imagining things?"

"Yes, now, tell me what you were—"

A pop sounded.

A hole appeared in the middle of his head.

I screamed and covered my head with my arms. No, wait. I was a sitting duck. There was no guessing whether the former chef was dead. No one survives a shot to the head. I scrambled through the bushes and took off as fast as I could.

When my heart threatened to beat out of my chest, I stopped. A twig snapped to my right. I fell to my knees.

"Whoa." A man in hunting gear parted the branches

above my head. "What are you doing out here? I could easily shoot you."

Oh, no. "Did you recently fire that gun?" I motioned toward his rifle.

"Yeah. Caught a glimpse of a deer. Thought you were another one."

"You shot a person!" I leaped to my feet and slammed both hands into his chest. "Idiot." I fished my cell phone from my pocket and dialed Matt's number. "We have another body. This one supposedly an accident." I gave him directions and yanked the hunter's sleeve. "Follow me."

"No. No. I didn't mean to. It was…" he whirled and crashed away, leaving me standing alone in an unfamiliar forest with a dead body mere yards away.

16

By the time Matt arrived in a golf cart, I had found my way to the road. Matt bent over Mom's crumpled body.

I rushed to her side. "Mom!" The thing I feared most had happened.

"Stormi." She covered her face and wept. "When I heard the gunshot, and you didn't appear, I feared the worst."

"I thought the same when I saw you here. The body is in there." I pointed before wrapping my arms around Mom. "Can we go home now?"

She took a deep, shuddering breath. "No. I promised the kids horseback riding and zip-lining. They've been very patient on this non-vacation of ours. They deserve some fun."

My shoulders slumped. I really didn't know how much more I could take. Couldn't we schedule those types of activities somewhere else? Somewhere death didn't taint the air?

I sat on the side of the road and waited what felt like hours for Matt to return. When he did, he squatted in front of us.

"What happened?" He smoothed the hair away from my face.

Instead of answering, I threw myself into his arms, driving him backwards. The breath left him in a whoosh as he landed hard on his backside. Answers could wait. I needed comfort. I wrapped my arms around his neck and held on like a drowning person.

"It's okay." He hugged me tight. "I won't let anything happen to you."

"You weren't here."

"You left without waiting for me."

"Never again."

He chuckled. "I've heard that before." He helped me to my feet and into the seat of the golf cart. "Want to tell me what happened?" His smile faded, and his expression turned grave.

I closed my eyes in an attempt not to forget anything. "I was questioning Bertolinni. He said someone shot at him outside the dormitory, but I didn't believe him. I thought he was paranoid. Then, we ducked into the woods, out of sight, me this way, Mom that, and someone shot him." Shudders overtook me and Matt draped his fleece hoodie around my shoulders. "I ran into a hunter. He said he had just killed a deer. When I told him he had shot a person, he took off."

Wayne and Rodriguez darted into the trees, presumably after the hunter.

"You and Anne take the cart," Matt said, placing a tender kiss on my forehead. "We'll walk back after the crime scene investigators are finished."

"Thank you." I didn't think my legs would hold me long enough to carry me that distance.

Mom climbed into the driver's seat. "I've always wanted to drive one of these." She placed a hand over mine. "I'm glad you aren't dead."

I laughed. "I'm glad you're still kicking, too."

"Great. Let's go eat." She started the ignition and sped toward the main building.

Food did not sound good at the moment, but maybe I'd

hear something of value. If Bertolinni's death wasn't an accident, only the killer would know he was dead. I was hoping someone would slip up and say something incriminating.

Fifteen minutes later, we were sitting at supper. The room was as loud and bustling as ever with Cheri watching over everyone like a queen on her throne. No one seemed to miss the former chef.

The group of bridesmaids giggled and hollered from a nearby table. They didn't seem to feel the absence of the bride in the slightest. Shelby probably demanded the attention be on her every minute and they could now enjoy themselves.

My family ate at a table to my left. Angela cast glares my way. Wait until she found out how close Mom and I had come to being shot. I bet her rare tender side toward me would show.

"Found this." Rusty plopped down at our table and handed me a matchbook from a restaurant in Australia.

"Where did you get this?"

"Bad woman's room."

"Thank you, but you should have left it to me."

He shook his head, his ridiculously over-sized bow tie dangling at his throat. "Too dangerous for a woman."

I chose the wise course of not arguing with him. His snooping had just proved Cheri had been in Australia. I slipped it into my pocket to show Matt when he returned. "Anything else?"

"Plane ticket." He grinned and handed it to me. "Rusty did good."

"Yes, you did." My face fell. The name on the ticket was Mason Lereux. He hadn't found new information at all. Still, I forced a smile, not wanting to steal his thunder.

Mom, obviously, had no such thought. "That's Shelby's

ticket. We need something against Cheri."

Rusty frowned. "This?" He handed me an itinerary for Lauren Boudreaux.

"Who in the world is this?" I had seen the name on the flight manifest, only noticing it because of the French sounding name.

"Bad woman."

"Why?"

He tossed a passport and driver's license on the table. Both had Cheri's picture and Lauren's name.

I opened the passport. A stamp showed she had gone to Australia under the name of Laureen at the same time Seth and Shelby had. I sat back in my seat, covering the items with my napkin. I'd bet my favorite pair of shoes that Cheri was the woman on the flight with the bad wig. But, why lie? If Cheri was the killer, why kill Seth and not Shelby? The web tangled further.

Mom took the items, napkin and all, and slid them into her purse. "Now what?"

"I have no idea." I bit my lower lip. "If Cheri is the killer, she'll flee. But, she has the opportunity to have done everything that's been happening. Is it possible she knows about the offshore accounts?"

"How?" Mom set her purse in her lap. "What relation does she have to Boyd Industries?"

"That's what we need to find out." Then, we could confront her and, possibly, put an end to this reign of madness.

Time for more research on the computer. I stood and motioned for Cherokee to follow me. As we made our way to the cottage, I filled my niece in on what I needed her to do.

"I'll do my best. I like digging into people's personal lives." She grinned. "Maybe you can hire me as your IT person for the investigative business."

"I'd be happy to, if I ever go that route full time. How are you feeling?"

"Better. The nightmares are less."

"Even with all that is happening here?"

"What is happening here doesn't directly affect me." She swiped her card into the lock and opened the cottage door.

"Age before beauty."

"You got that ri—" I froze. The place looked as if a tornado blew through.

Cushions ripped apart. Dishes shattered. The sofa had been slashed and suitcases dumped. Written in red across one wall were the words, "Go home".

"Find those financial forms." If they were gone, we were back at square one.

"Heavens to Betsy!" Mom stood in the doorway.

I whirled. "Tell me you have those offshore accounts." The police department did, but I felt better having a copy where we could do our own investigating.

"Of course, I do." She patted the big bag she called a purse. "They've been here since day one. I stashed an extra copy in my bra too. Best hiding place in the world, although it is a bit scratchy. I doubt anyone will go looking there."

I sagged with relief to the ruined sofa and reached for my laptop. Since it was password protected, it seemed to be in good condition. I handed it to Cherokee. "Work your magic while I call Matt."

Poor man. I kept him running from one corner of the resort to the other. Some recuperation for his shoulder. I dialed Matt's number.

"Please don't tell me you have another body," he said.

"Nope, just a ransacked cottage."

"We'll be there within the hour. Don't leave and lock the door. Don't touch anything. Keep your gun close at hand."

Having my gun either in my waistband or in my purse

was becoming second nature. We traded "I love you" and hung up. Not being able to clean the mess around me, I watched Cherokee's fingers fly across the keyboard of the laptop.

"Finding anything?"

"It takes more than two minutes."

I sighed and got up to lock the door, waiting while my sister, nephew, and Maryann entered. "Welcome to hell."

Maryann shook her head. "What a mess." She dropped her purse on the table. "While you were off creating trouble, I've spent some time eavesdropping on our group of bridesmaids. Want to know what I heard?"

"Please." I took her hand and led her to the kitchen table. After standing a couple of chairs back on four legs, we sat down. "Spill."

"Shelby's engagement is off. Lawrence, not being a suspect, has left the resort." She looked pleased with herself. "He paid another week's worth of resort fee for her and left a screaming Shelby in the love nest they once shared."

This was news. "Did they say why they broke up?"

"Supposedly, the big man can't take the drama. He said the world is full of beautiful women, and he'll find one more to his liking as the wife of an important person. Needless to say, Shelby is beside herself and being restrained in the clinic for threatening suicide."

"I didn't know the resort had a clinic." The waters continued to be muddied.

"Cheri is Shelby's cousin," Cherokee said, turning the laptop around so I could see. "She changed her name two years ago to Cheri Mason and bragged on Facebook how she lost her accent."

"She's here on a work visa?"

"Looks that way." Cherokee held out her hand. "Twenty-five bucks, please."

"But, I—fine." I took the money from my purse. It was inexpensive as far as consulting fees went.

The sound of the door unlocking drew our attention. I pulled my gun from my purse and stood ready, lowering my guard when Matt, Wayne, and Rodriguez entered. After all, whoever had ransacked the room had had a card key. I could testify to how easy they were to obtain.

Rodriguez glared at me, then made his way from room-to-room while I quietly filled Matt in on what Maryann and Cherokee had discovered. "What did you find out in the woods?"

"Why are we whispering?" he asked.

"I don't trust him." I motioned my head toward the bedroom.

"Smart girl." He tweaked my nose. "Bertolinni's death was no accident. We found where the shooter knelt in the woods. He had a clear line of sight to where the two of you were standing." A shadow passed over his eyes. "If you hadn't of run and tried to call me…"

My blood drained to my feet. "I can identify the shooter, Matt." I gripped his arms. "I looked into his face."

17

The next morning, I put my foot in the stirrup of a handsome horse the color of Arkansas clay and hoisted myself into the saddle, making sure Matt was nearby. I hadn't been kidding when I said I wanted him by my side every minute from now on.

"What's this beauty's name?" I asked the guide.

"JR. You'll have to show him who is boss. He might be small, but he's feisty." Barb, our guide, slapped JR on the rump. "Move him up. He refuses to have any horse in front of him, but mine."

Mom was right. Squeezing in a few more days of fun before heading back home was just what we needed. The sun shined bright, a cool breeze kept us from getting too hot on an unnaturally warm fall day, and birds serenaded us from the nearby trees. I grinned at Matt over my shoulder.

He returned the smile and held his large black horse's reins loosely in his good hand. "You should have ridden with me. Your arms around my waist is just what I need."

While the gesture was sweet, I enjoyed riding alone. "Ride next to me."

The moment he moved closer, JR tried to take a bite of inky dark horseflesh. I shrugged as Matt fell in behind me.

Once everyone was on horseback, Barb mounted her chestnut roan and led us away from the resort and across a meadow. Bulging saddlebags behind her saddle held our lunch.

"When we head home on Friday," I tossed over my shoulder, "is Rodriguez going to pursue the investigation on his own?"

"I'll probably stay behind," Matt said. "I'm with you in not trusting him. Either the man is as dumb as that tree or he's dirty. Either way, I'm needed here. I'll send Wayne home with you."

"Can't it be the other way around?" I twisted in the saddle.

"And incur your sister's wrath? No, thank you. I'd love to be the one to go home with you, but my captain elected me to stay behind."

I wasn't worried that Wayne couldn't protect us. I knew first hand what he would do to make sure we stayed alive. Still, I'd worry every moment about Matt left behind.

"This isn't the first time there has been trouble at Mountain Springs," Barb said. "I might not be an employee there, having stuck to my independent trail rides, but I hear things. Last year, that snobby manager was in a bit of financial trouble. Word is…she has an online gambling problem. She was overcharging for the cottages and pocketing the difference. Corporation found out and gave her a warning. Stop or get out."

I felt as if I'd had a palm slap to the forehead. "Is Mountain Springs owned by Boyd Industries?"

"Yep." She led us out of the open and into the trees.

I glanced back at Matt and raised my eyebrows. He nodded, his face grim.

Guess who became our number one suspect? I drew in a sharp breath. What if Cheri and Shelby were in cahoots with each other? Blood ran deep in the Ozarks, and they were family. Even with the ongoing rivalry between me and

Angela, we could harass each other, but no one else better dare.

J.R. danced under me every time another horse got close. I enjoyed horses that were plodding old dodgers, but this rambunctious animal showed me it wouldn't do to lose my concentration.

"Settle down, boy." I gave the reins a gentle tug. "You're going to give me blisters on my behind."

"It looks like your saddle is slipping," Matt said. "Hold up."

Barb halted the line and slid from the back of her horse. "Let me take a look."

J.R. hopped sideways. My saddle tilted. The next thing I knew, I was on the ground studying the horse's belly. I curled into a ball and covered my head.

The horse moved to the side and blew hot breath on the back of my head. I reached up and pushed him away.

"Are you all right?" Matt helped me to my feet.

Barb grabbed J.R.'s reins and ran her hands down his quivering flank. "There's a notch cut out of the cinch. I've got a temporary fix, but I suggest you take your boyfriend up on riding double." Her face darkened. "I'm so sorry. This has never happened before."

"That's because I wasn't riding one of your horses before." I dusted off the back of my jeans. It was an accident, right? No one could have known which horse I would ride, unless it didn't matter which of our group got injured. I had a feeling someone wanted us gone by any means necessary. I gave myself a mental shake.

Falling from the horse rarely killed a person, unless they struck their head on a rock. I gave the rocks on the side of the trail a dirty look. "It's called the Stormi syndrome. I'll be fine." Bruised maybe, but still moving.

"I got my wish after all." Matt got back on his horse and

held a hand down to swing me up behind him.

I wrapped my arm around his waist and breathed deep of his cologne and a scent that was all Matt. Something masculine and sexy with a hint of musk. Only my man could ride a horse and still smell good.

"Are you sure you aren't hurt?" He asked.

"I'm fine. Clumsiness is my middle name, remember?"

He made a noise in his throat. "I'm glad you weren't hurt."

"An accident, right?"

He shrugged. "No way to prove otherwise."

I stiffened. "You don't think so?"

"With you? You attract trouble like cops to a doughnut shop."

I exhaled sharply. "Well, if it was planned, I'm glad it was me and not Mom."

"I heard that," Mom called out. "You'd think I was old and brittle the way you go on."

Barb led us to a clearing next to a bubbling creek. "We'll stop here for an hour. The water is shallow, but icy cold, if anyone wants to wade."

Dakota and Cherokee were the first to take their shoes off and were soon splashing each other and shrieking. I couldn't wait to join in the fun.

My feet went numb the moment I stepped into the water. It didn't take long, though, for me to disregard the sharp cold and wade in as far as I could roll up my pant legs. Didn't take but a second more for Dakota to send a wave of ice water at my face.

"You do know it's October, right? Not July. I'm going to freeze to death." Hair that had escaped my ponytail stuck to my face. I turned and trudged back to the bank. Let the kids catch a chill.

"Spoil sport," he said, laughing. "Cherokee and I don't

mind the cold."

I sniffed. They were kids. I was an adult and had more sense. Still barefoot, I helped Mom unload the lunch while Matt and Wayne conversed quietly at the edge of the water, occasionally scanning the line of trees. Rusty, afraid of horses, had elected to stay behind at the resort. I prayed he was watching television in the cottage like he promised.

Barb cared for the horses, clearly upset over my fall. Nothing I said eased her guilt. Maybe a thick ham and cheese sandwich would help.

"Lunch." I held out the paper towel wrapped sandwich.

"I'm not hungry."

"It wasn't your fault, Barb." I offered the food again. "Really. These things happen to me all the time."

Her shoulders slumped. "You've been through so much, according to the grapevine. I wanted the ride to be a pleasant experience."

"It is. I'm enjoying myself. The others are, too. Eat."

She took the sandwich. "Thank you." She perched on a fallen log, face downcast.

I rejoined the others and sat on a corner of a quilt spread across a carpet of autumn leaves. I wished the men would relax, but couldn't blame them for standing guard. Not after the so-called vacation we'd had so far. Still, the beauty of the day covered the ugliness.

After I ate, I laid down, watching clouds converge overhead. It looked like rain. Wonderful. That was one thing that could definitely put a damper on the day. I didn't relish arriving back at the resort, cold and shivering.

An increasing wind disturbed the water of the creek and rustled tree branches. Barb told us to pack up and cut the lunch break short. We had to head back.

I went to sit up, only to have my head jerked back. "Ow!" I grabbed my hair and turned. J.R. had my ponytail in his mouth. "He's eating my hair!"

"That horse is going to be the death of me." Barb grabbed his reins. "He's worse than a child. There is no keeping him tethered. I can't put him in the same corral as the other horses because he's always picking fights." She freed me and led the horse away.

"What's the damage?" I showed Mom my hair.

"A little uneven on the ends," she said. "Nothing a good stylist can't fix."

I vowed then and there to schedule another vacation as soon as possible. One with no murders, thefts, a hair-eating horse, or a crime of any kind. I yanked the blanket from the ground and rolled it into a tube before handing it to Barb to tie onto J.R. If no one was going to ride him, he might as well pull his weight another way.

Thunder rumbled in the distance seconds before fat raindrops fell.

"There's a cave this way," Barb said. "Everyone grab something and a horse's reins. It isn't far, but we'll have to lead the animals." She stepped into the rising creek and led the way across.

Seriously? In one hand, I still carried my shoes, in the other, J.R.'s reins. I glared at the horse. "Behave. I don't like this any more than you do."

I once again stepped into the freezing water, no longer able to keep my pants dry. The water rose to mid-thigh.

J.R. splashed behind me, soaking my back. He snorted against my neck. I swore he tormented me on purpose.

I yelped, losing my footing. The water closed over my head and stole my breath. The only thing that kept me from being swept away was my firm grip on the reins. Instead of me leading the horse, he dragged me to the opposite shore, staying true to having to be at the front of the line.

Struggling to my feet, I smacked his rump. "Beast." I

marched past him and into a cave. Good. Someone had the foresight to stockpile a load of wood against one wall.

"We keep wood and a lantern here for times like this," Barb said. "Tie the reins to a tree outside. The poor horses will have to make do until the rain stops."

"I'll get a fire started," Wayne offered. "Of course, the expression on Stormi's face might get a flame going before these matches."

"Very funny. I'm freezing." The quilt I had carefully tied to the back of J.R.'s saddle was sopping wet and no good to me now.

Matt wrapped his good arm around me and rested his chin on my head. "I'll warm you up."

I sighed and nestled back against him. "Why does anything bad that's going to happen, always happen to me?"

"Luck."

"Lack thereof, you mean."

"It's fodder for your stories."

"True." I turned and kissed him. "You always know what to say."

Wayne soon had a tiny fire going. I stepped away from Matt and crouched next to the flames, welcoming the warmth.

Lightning cracked overhead. A tree fell across the opening of the cave. The horses whinnied and yanked free before racing away.

I sighed and held my hands closer to the blaze. Fodder for my stories, indeed.

"Don't worry," Barb said. "They'll return as soon as the storm is over. They know who feeds them."

Wayne straightened. "I'll get started breaking up that branch so we can get out when it's time." He laughed. "You, drowned red rat, are bad luck."

Wasn't I though?

18

Night had fallen by the time we trudged to our cottage. Although I was no longer soaking wet, I was far from completely dry, and couldn't wait to take a hot shower and wrap in a fluffy robe.

"I'm bushed, babe." Matt planted a kiss on my lips. "I'll stop by in the morning, okay?"

I nodded. "I plan on going straight to bed."

We kissed again, and he leaned his forehead against mine while the others trooped past us. "We need to hurry and get married," he said, "so we don't have to go to separate rooms."

"Agree. Let's finalize a date as soon as we—"

"She's gone." Mom bustled up to us.

"Who?" I sighed and stepped back.

"Cheri. Rusty said she packed her bags and left while we were gone."

I wanted to dance a jig. We could enjoy the last couple of days of our vacation with no worries. Her running off cinched the fact she was the murderer. She was probably on a flight to Mexico, or back to France, this very minute.

"I need to call Rodriguez," Matt told me. "I'll talk to you in the morning. I love you."

"Ditto." I watched until he entered his cottage. "I'm getting married, Mom."

"Obviously. That's why you're wearing a ring."

"I mean soon. We're setting a date as soon as we get home."

"A spring wedding. Perfect."

"No, Christmas." I put my arm around her shoulders and stepped into the cottage with her. "I don't want to wait."

"Finally, we can have some fun," Angela said. "We leave in three days, and I've done nothing but rattle around here."

"If you call daily massages and facials rattling around, you've had a rough time of things, for sure." I thanked Rusty and sent him on his way, glad more than I could say that he had stowed away in Matt's truck. His peeping where he wasn't wanted paid off more times than I could count.

After a hot shower, I fell asleep dreaming of Matt, weddings, and home.

I woke to a pounding on my bedroom door. I cracked one eye open and stared across the room at Maryann, who stuffed a pillow over her head.

"I'm coming in," Mom said. "Don't worry about being decent, I've seen it all before."

Not since she changed my diapers, but who cared? "Come in. I'm up."

"Get dressed. The chef is gone, too, and there are a lot of hungry people in the restaurant. We're cooking."

"Wait. What?" I flung back the blankets.

"With Cheri gone, employees are leaving left and right. If we want to eat, we have to cook." She frowned down at me. "It isn't something we haven't done before."

True, but let a girl wake up before throwing something of that magnitude at her. "I'll be there in fifteen minutes."

I made it in twenty. I stumbled into the commercial style kitchen and stared. It was everything a cook could ever want. I might only cook when stressed, and my full freezer at home could testify that I was stressed over my latest book quite a lot, but I was definitely knee deep in envy. "This isn't going to be work. This will be a vacation!" I tied a crisp one apron over my clothes.

"Let's see if you still feel that way after filling the breakfast buffet," Mom said. "We need scrambled eggs, sausage, bacon, cut up fruit, pancakes…You name it, we got to fix it."

"No, we don't. We make a gourmet breakfast and let Rusty carry it out. The guests can take it or leave it." I rubbed my hands together. "This is a survival situation." I couldn't be happier.

"I already sent Matt and Wayne out to take omelet orders." Mom cracked eggs into a bowl.

"Fine." Why couldn't she do things the easy way for once? "I'll work on the omelets. You, Angela, Maryann, and Cherokee each take something else. Dakota, you have kitchen duty."

He groaned. "I knew it."

"Just stack them on that belt and push the button." Did I mention I was jealous?

"Cool." He sat in a chair to wait for the first load. "Do you think the guests will give me a tip if I bus their table?"

"I doubt it. The meals are included in the cost."

For the next hour, I made omelets like a crazed scientist, before collapsing, happy but exhausted, into a nearby chair. Before taking up writing, I'd entertained the idea of being a chef. It might be fun once in a while, but I felt like I'd been run over by a truck.

"Thank you." A clapping drew my attention to the kitchen door. Shelby, dressed in a navy suit, beamed. "I'm the acting manager and I must say, bravo!"

Oh, good grief. I slumped in my seat. Just when I was ready to relax.

"I really had no idea what we were going to do.

Rodriguez refuses to let the bridesmaids leave. Said he is still investigating. Isn't that the weirdest thing? I've never heard of suspects being detained on a resort before. Guess there is always a first." She shrugged one shoulder. "Somebody has to feed them. I'm glad you're staying on to do so."

"No, no, no, no." I pushed to my feet. "We are leaving on Saturday. No exceptions. Y'all can fend for yourselves."

"Please." She clasped her hands together as if praying. "I can't cook."

"We'll cook until we leave." Mom tossed a dish towel onto the counter. "We have a zip-lining appointment tomorrow, and we're leaving after breakfast the next day. We can leave a couple of meals in the freezer for you. I'm sure you'll be released soon enough. With Cheri flying the coop, she as much as admitted her guilt."

"She's right," Matt said, squeezing past Shelby and into the room. "Rodriguez said once everyone is gone, you're free to go. You can kick everyone out now, if you want to."

My family started yelling at once. Clearly, no one wanted to miss zipping through the trees covered with autumn foliage.

Shelby looked relieved. "By midday Saturday, this place will be nothing more than a ghost town. The only ones left are y'all and the wedding party. Even the servants have gone. There is no reason for me to stay." She turned and left.

"I had no idea she would still work for Boyd Industries after Lawrence broke off their engagement," I said.

Mom shrugged. "A gal's gotta make a living."

"I suppose." I glanced at the others. "Take a few hours off. Mom and I will plan sandwiches for lunch, and find something for dinner. No personal orders, though. Everyone eats the same meal."

"With no staff left, what are we supposed to do?" Angela planted fists on her hips.

"I have no idea." Nor, did I care. There was nothing more relaxing than to do nothing. Which is exactly what I planned on doing as soon as the day's meals were planned.

When everyone had left, Mom and I headed for the freezer to take inventory. I pulled a clip from the hinge and opened the heavy metal door. "What a waste." The shelves of the eight by ten foot room was filled.

"What do you think they'll do with it all when they close the resort?"

I shrugged. "Maybe they won't close it. Maybe they'll hire all new staff and be up and running within a couple of weeks." I hoped so. If there hadn't have been a murder, it really was a nice place to spend a week…or two.

"We could do chicken parmesan." Mom stepped on a stool. "If we take these chicken breasts out now, they should thaw in time."

The door slammed shut.

I pushed against it. Nothing. "Will we thaw by then?" I cupped my hands and peered through the small window in the door. "Uh, Mom. We're locked in."

"Impossible. These doors have protection against that."

"Take a look. There's no protection against someone putting the chain through the lock." I wrapped my arms around me. How long could we last in there? How long until someone missed us?

"Okay, don't panic." Mom rattled the handle. When that didn't work, she kicked the door. "Help! Let us out! We're going to freeze in here."

"Don't panic, huh?" I glanced around. There was one way in, or out, and it was locked. Maybe we were wrong about Cheri or Shelby being our killer. Suddenly, staying until Saturday lost its appeal.

"There are a couple of those packing blankets in the corner." I grabbed one and tossed it to Mom, wrapping another around my shoulders. "It will help for a while."

"Great idea. One of the others is bound to come looking for us soon. We'll keep knocking occasionally, until they do." She sat on the stool. "Wait. Your phone?"

"On the counter."

"Mine, too. Now, what?"

"We wait. We've been in tough spots before."

"Yeah, like a burning basement." Mom twisted her lips. "Or an old shack where we were held at gunpoint. And the time we were tied up in the back of a van. We got out of those spots, we'll get out of this. How often do you think those things can happen to people before their luck runs out?"

"I'd rather not think about that, if you don't mind."

"You're right. Let's think about something pleasant, like your wedding."

"Are you sure? I want a Christmas wedding. It's cold at Christmas."

"Let's pretend you're having it in July." Mom shivered. "On a beach during a heat wave. Your lips are turning blue."

I supposed there were worse ways to die. I'd read somewhere that freezing to death was kind of like falling asleep. My head bobbed forward.

Mom slapped me. "Stay awake, Stormi." She got up to bang on the door. After knocking and kicking it a couple of times, she sat back down, then bolted to her feet. "Let's walk."

We paced in a circle, stomping to keep the blood circulating. Each touch of my foot to the floor sent shards of pain up my leg. My nose felt as if it would fall off if someone touched it. Where was my family? Why hadn't Matt missed me?

"How long do you think we've been in here?" Mom asked.

"Forever."

"Seriously."

"About an hour, maybe more." I leaned against the wall and glanced at the window in the door.

Blessed Rusty. He peered in, then seconds later the door opened. "You were locked in."

"Yes, we were." I wrapped my arms around him and squeezed. "Thank you."

"Matt told me to come get you. He wants to sit in the hot tub and sip champagne."

"That sounds wonderful. Tell him I want a hot coffee."

"Okay." He dashed away.

Before we made it back to the cottage, Matt and Wayne came running. Matt scooped me into his arms, blanket and all, and raced for the cottage. "We'll do the hot tub later. You're getting in the shower right now."

I was too spent to argue. I wanted to ask him if anyone had seen Cheri skulking around, but even that took more energy than I had.

While Wayne handed Mom over to Angela's care, Maryann took over for Matt. She turned on the shower, then helped me strip. "Are you sure you don't want to soak in the tub?"

"One word." My eyes widened. "Jellyfish."

She rolled her eyes. "I'd fix the bath. The window is closed."

"I'm still not taking the chance. With my luck, something would crawl up the drain."

"With the stopper in?" The look she gave me told me I was being ridiculous, and I didn't care. I was not taking another bath while at the resort.

Within minutes, I was standing in a hot shower, each drop sending pricks of heat burning through me as my body tingled back to life. It had been a close call. But, as Mom stated, we'd been in tough situations before.

If God continued to send help, we wouldn't have to worry about our luck running out. Not until He called us home, which I hoped was not for a very long time.

19

I stared at a wooden ladder that led to a platform nestled in the branches of a massive oak tree. Why did it have to stretch so high? I'd be perfectly happy zipping through the trees six feet above the ground. It's the speed that's the thrill, right?

"Scared?" Dakota grinned and scampered past me and up the ladder.

"Come on." Matt slipped off his sling. "I'll be right behind you."

"Maybe we shouldn't. You're still healing. I wouldn't want you to rip out your stitches." I bit my bottom lip.

"I'm willing to chance it. I've never been zip-lining. It'll be fun." He nudged me closer to the ladder.

"Can we ride double?"

He laughed. "Get up there. Look, Dakota is going."

I tilted my head back to see my nephew step off the platform and go flying. "That doesn't help."

I gripped the bottom rung and climbed, my heart in my throat. I'd never considered myself afraid of heights, but this put things in a new perspective.

The view took my breath away more than the height. A forest of gold, pumpkin and crimson stretched before me. Limestone cliffs rose to kiss the sky. In the distance, I could see the second platform and Dakota landing as his sister jumped into the air for her turn.

Angela shrieked when it was her turn, and screamed all the way to the platform. I could do better. Not a sound would pass my lips. I'd be so engrossed in the scenery, and choked with fear, if it were possible to do both at the same time.

All too soon it was my turn. I stared at Matt while the line operator strapped me into my harness.

"This is the brake," he said. "Squeeze if you're going too fast, and definitely squeeze before hitting the next platform or you'll zip on by and crash into someone."

Oh, Lord. I reached for Matt.

"Remember. I'm right behind you."

"It isn't as if you can climb out to me if I get stuck."

"Of course, I will."

"No," the operator said, shaking his head. "That would be too dangerous. She'll have to make sure she keeps going."

Holy cow, I was going to have a heart attack. "Push me." I teetered on the edge.

"Jump," Matt said.

"No, you have to push me. I'm frozen. My feet are glued to the woo—ah!" I screamed until my throat hurt as he planted his hands against my back and gave me a shove.

"Squeeze the brake!" The guy on the opposite platform waved his arms.

Oh, right. I squeezed and coasted onto the platform. "That was kind of fun."

"Try enjoying it next time," he said. "Ready?"

I nodded, told him to push me, and flew. It was exhilarating. I slowed to a respectable speed that allowed me to look around. "Hello, bear!" I waved at a black bear standing on its hind legs, its mouth full of grass. That wasn't a sight you saw every day. I could swear he waved back.

My harness gave a lurch. Turbulence? It kind of felt like when an airplane hit rough areas in the sky. It did it again and felt myself drop. I glanced upward. The line was fraying. I glanced down. A creek full of rocks and white rushing water swept by. I was going to die.

"Matt!" I kicked my feet, then froze. Movement would only cause the rope to fray faster. If I could reach…I stretched my arm toward the cable over my head. If I could get higher, and straddle the cable, maybe I could inch my way to safety. I dropped another inch and screamed.

I couldn't blame anyone else on my predicament, could I? No one could have known which harness I would take. Unless, the killer hired one of the operators to mess with my equipment. Was I that paranoid?

I let go of the brake and grabbed the line above me with one hand, pulling myself closer to the cable overhead. When I could grasp it, I swung my other hand up, grabbed hold, and hung there like a monkey. Now what?

The line sagged. I glanced over to see Matt moving toward me. "Go back! It won't hold our weight."

"You can't hold on for long."

As if his words were all the weight my line needed, it snapped. I plummeted downward, swinging like Tarzan at the end of a vine. At least there were safety precautions in place.

"Hold still," Matt called.

"I'm doing my best. Kind of hard when I'm swinging back and forth." I clutched the straps of my harness as if that alone would save me. Lord have mercy, one of the operators was now on the cable. How much weight could it hold?

My line jerked up, then a bit more. I glanced overhead. Matt and the other guy were reeling me up likc a giant fish. Relief washed over me. Better to go up, than down, although my harness was cutting into my inner thighs and chafing my skin.

I glanced into Matt's face. "Can we go home now?"

He nodded, his face grave. "I think that's best." He reached down a hand.

I latched on, trying not to think how much hauling me up had hurt him. The operator tied a second line to my harness and hand-over-hand, they dragged me to the platform. Solid ground, such as it was, had never felt so good.

Refusing to go another foot by zip line, I scuttled down the long ladder until I was firmly on dirt and leaves. The others could finish the ride and meet us at the van. As for me, I'd never hiked through the forest as fast as I did that morning.

I leaned against the driver's side door and took deep breaths. "I need to be in a padded cage. It's the only way I'll stay out of trouble."

Matt chuckled, pulling me into his arms. "I'm starting to think the same thing. I wanted to take a cruise for our honeymoon, but with your luck, the ship would sink."

"Ha ha." I wanted to stay in his arms forever, but the voices of my returning family signaled we were no longer alone. "Don't tell them what happened."

"Why not?"

"They don't need to be worried about a disaster that was averted." I stepped back and forced a smile to my face.

"How did you get here before us?" Mom asked, searching our faces.

"We didn't go the whole route," I said. "A short distance was enough for me." I turned away so Mom couldn't see my lie. I'd never been good at telling false tales. "Let's go back and pack. We're heading home tonight."

"There's something you aren't telling me." Mom opened the back of the van and tossed a backpack inside. "I'll get it out of you soon enough. You look like you've had the fright of your life, and Matt's shoulder is bleeding."

Guilt, so raw it hurt, washed over me. "Let it be, Mom."

"Okay." Her feelings were hurt, but there was nothing I could do.

After all that had happened over the course of the last two weeks, I wouldn't pile more on her head. We'd go home, return to what was normal, and forget all about our so-called vacation. The only good thing that came out of it all was the return of Cherokee's smile and the color to her face.

We drove back to the resort, surprised to see Shelby and the bridesmaids almost packing up to leave. Shelby told us no one had the heart to stay any longer and that Boyd Industries had refunded our entire two week stay.

That was good news. Inside the cottage, I made the rounds, making sure we left nothing behind. In the bedroom I'd shared with Maryann, I stared at the tub. How easy it had been for someone to kill a man relaxing in his bubble bath.

According to Rusty, Cheri hadn't made an appearance since leaving, and Rodriguez said they'd called in the FBI to help locate her. Good. I was finished with this mystery. It turned out to be more than my inexperienced hands could handle. Unfortunately, Matt still had to stay nearby to help. There were times I wished I'd fallen in love with an accountant.

I chose to drive, leaving Mom to sulk in the passenger seat while the others, minus Wayne, Rusty, and Dakota, climbed in the back. The men would follow us.

The sky decided to pour rivers of water on our vans as we pulled out of the resort and headed down the mountain. At least it had waited until after my horrific zip-lining experience. I couldn't imagine dangling over a river in a downpour, or having Matt and a young man barely out of college dangle above me.

"This is a fitting send-off," Mom said. "This has not been the vacation I thought it would be. We did have some fun, but it was always ruined somehow."

"Not the facials or massages." Angela poked her head between us. "We at least had that."

"The zip-lining was fun," Cherokee added. "And the hike and horseback riding. It wasn't all a total waste."

She should have seen the excursions through my eyes. I glanced in the rearview mirror. "I'm glad to see you happy again. That makes everything worth it."

She smiled and sat back. "Can you see out the windshield? That rain is coming down hard."

Mom's cell phone rang. "It's Wayne. Hello, dear. You think so? Okay, but we really want to get—look out!"

A river of mud raced down the mountain, bringing rocks and boulders the size of a Volkswagen Beetle down and over the road. I slammed on the brakes, fishtailing the van, before coming to a stop. A rock banged into Mom's door.

"Wayne was calling to tell us to pull over until the rain let up. I guess that problem is solved," she said.

Wow. I glanced out my window at the canyon to my left. Spared that catastrophe at least.

Wayne trudged through the rain and knocked on my window. "Everyone all right?"

"Yes," I shouted through the glass. "Looks like we're stuck until someone clears the road."

He nodded. "I'll make the call now." He dashed back to his vehicle.

I rested my head against the back of my seat. Another close call that day. I closed my eyes. *Lord, what are you trying to teach me?*

I revisited the scene where the police knocked on our door to tell us someone had shot Dad while he walked home from work. I rarely thought about that night. After months of investigating, his death was considered unsolvable, and written off as a transient looking for money. His file was put into storage. At first, I thought seeking justice for others was what drove me into solving these crimes. Now, I thought maybe I was a bit deranged. Getting justice for others would not bring Dad back. I doubted it would even help soothe the pain of losing him.

Yes, writing books about the crimes was filling my bank account, but if I were dead, I wouldn't be able to enjoy the fruits of my labors. It was time to seriously rethink my life.

Starting with the PI badge in my purse.

20

I groaned and stretched my arms above my head. Home. What a wonderful word.

Sadie laid her massive head on my bed and stared at me with big black eyes. I reached over and scratched behind her left ear. "I missed you, girl. Where are the cats?"

As if they'd heard and understood, Ebony and Ivory pounced on the bed and curled up next to me. My neighbors, the Salazars, had done a wonderful job of caring for my babies. I'd cook them a casserole as thanks.

Sadie turned her head and sniffed. I did the same. Bacon! I rolled out of bed. "Come on, girl, it's time for breakfast."

"Good morning!" I sang as I hugged Mom.

"You're awfully chipper this morning."

"No more psycho resort managers." I poured a cup of coffee and leaned against the counter. "Are you upset you didn't get to cook more meals in that wonderful kitchen?"

"Not after getting locked in the freezer. I thought that was the end of us." She slid an omelet onto a plate and handed it to me. "Bacon is on the table."

"Not anymore. Sadie, get down!" She stood tall enough all it took was the flick of a tongue and food was gone.

Mom laughed. "There's more in the microwave."

"Thank goodness." I glared at my giant Irish Wolfhound. "Go lay down. You've had your treat. Are the others still

137

sleeping?"

"The kids are. Angela decided to go into work with Wayne." Mom brought her plate to the table and sat across from me. "This was one mystery we weren't able to solve."

I shrugged. "A gal can't win them all."

"But it's nice to do so." Mom cut her omelet into bite size pieces, then laid her fork next to her plate. "I have a hard time believing she simply disappeared. Cheri really seemed to want those account numbers."

"Where are they now?"

"The safe."

I agreed with Mom. It was strange that Cheri took off without the items she had killed for. I stared out the window as a shiver ran down my spine. I had the awful feeling things weren't over yet.

Still, work called. I had a book to write, whether we knew the ending or not. I was an author. I made stuff up.

"Are you going into work today?" I asked.

"Yes. Greta has handled the bakery alone long enough. She texted me and said we had a wedding to cater. They want cupcakes."

We ate the rest of our breakfast in silence, then Mom left Cherokee and Dakota a note telling them where she'd gone. "Good luck with the writing," she said, grabbing her purse on the way out.

I set the alarm and headed for my office. Emails tended to pile up when I was gone.

I booted my laptop and sighed. Over a thousand. Half an hour later, I had deleted the obvious ones I didn't need to respond to, answered one from my agent, reminding me I needed to start thinking of promotion for my new release next month. My fingers froze over the keyboard at the last unanswered message. The title read that it was from the resort.

Why would they be emailing me? I'd paid my bill in full. I clicked to open it. Maybe it was my refund.

Nope. I peered closer at my screen. "Give me what I want or else." Hmm. No signature, but it didn't take a genius to know it was probably from Cheri. I hit delete. Unless further instructions came, there was nothing more I could do.

Words weren't coming either. After staring at a blank Word document, I decided I needed a cup of my friend's frozen coffee. I clipped Sadie's leash to her collar and headed to Main Street.

The fifteen minute walk through familiar, safe streets, did a lot for my outlook. I secured Sadie to a lamppost and pushed open the door to Delicious Aroma. As usual, Norma wasn't in her office, but seated behind a round table.

"Hello, stranger," she said with a grin. "How was vacation?" She motioned to her son, the Barista, to bring me my usual.

"A nightmare." I spent the next few minutes filling her in on the last two weeks. "I need a vacation from vacation."

"You do manage to find trouble, don't you?" She shook her head. "Things have been quiet around here, but that's probably because you were gone." She winked.

"I'd tell you to shut up, but you're right. I have a cloud of doom over my head. Matt stayed behind, boss's orders, to help local police." I leaned my elbows on the table. "I don't think they'll find the killer. If I was a betting woman, I'd say she followed us home. She might have gotten here before us."

"Now, who's paranoid?"

I straightened to receive my coffee. "I'm serious. I have something she wants. Why wouldn't she come to where I live in a last desperate attempt to retrieve it?"

"Be careful." She reached across and placed her hand over mine. "I worry about you."

"I think everyone does. Poor Matt. I'm surprised he doesn't have a head full of gray hair by now." I gave her a quick hug. "I'm going to see how Mom is settling back into work. Catch you tomorrow."

I retrieved Sadie and retied her to another pole across the street in front of Heavenly Bakes. When I entered, Mom was telling Greta of our adventures. As an ex-police officer, Mom's baking partner usually had insights we missed.

"Girl." Greta gathered me against her ample bosom. "You are something else."

I held up my hands. "I had nothing to do with this. A man was killed, his wife hired me to find his killer, she died…voila! Disaster."

"Have a cupcake." Greta handed me a chocolate on chocolate piece of heaven.

"Don't mind if I do." I took a bite and closed my eyes in sheer pleasure. "Your baking puts things back into perspective. If you could find a way to send this across the world, everyone would be at peace."

"Oh, go on." She paused. "No, really, go on. It isn't every day a woman hears words of praise."

I laughed. "I think I might be able to write something now. Just needed to walk these streets I love so much and taste heaven. See you at home later, Mom."

"Stay out of trouble."

"I'll do my best." I stepped outside. Now, where was that dog? I lifted her leash, which looked chewed through. It wasn't like her not to stay where I'd left her. "Sadie!"

I turned right toward the diner. Maybe her nose led her to the alley where she could scrounge in the garbage. I called her name again, trailing her leash behind me. When half an hour passed, I grew angry. When an hour had gone by, I got worried. Sadie might not listen if she saw a squirrel, but for the most part she was very obedient.

Being a mystery writer, my mind veered off in directions far from calming. What if she had been run over by a truck? What if someone snatched her for lab experiments? I sagged onto the bench in front of the drugstore. What was I going to do? I didn't know where else to look.

Seth Bridges, the pharmacist, and Betty Rogers, my one time nemesis and now wary friend, exited the drugstore. "What's wrong?" Betty planted herself in front of me.

"My dog is gone."

"Write a country song." She cackled. "Oh, you're serious. That big beast of yours is missing?"

I nodded. "I've looked everywhere."

"Not everywhere, or you would have found her." She tapped Seth on the shoulder. "Gather a posse. We need to find a hound."

His thick eyebrows almost disappeared into his hairline. "For a dog?"

"For a friend." She crossed her arms and glared.

"Okay." He headed back into the store.

"Thank you." I blinked back tears.

"Don't start crying. You're made of tough stuff. Buck up and pound the pavement. We'll meet you at the park in an hour."

The park! Why hadn't I looked there? I took off at a run, stopping next to the fountain in the center of the park. "Sadie!"

Slowly, the townspeople trickled to the park, eager to help. My heart almost exploded with gratitude. I know Sadie was only a dog, but she was my dog, and these were my people.

Mrs. Rogers took charge like an army sergeant, barking orders. "Call her name every few feet. Toss out treats if you have to, but don't bring home any strays. Stormi wants her dog, not a replacement." She waved her arms, and the crowd scattered. "Don't worry," she said, turning to me. "We'll find her. They always come home when they're hungry."

I hoped so. "I'll head home and search the woods behind my house. Maybe she went there and caught scent of something."

"I'll call you later. Don't worry. I have everything under control."

I had no doubt.

Weariness threatened to choke me by the time I got home. Dakota and Cherokee met me on the porch, having been phoned by Mrs. Rogers.

"We'll find her," Dakota said, putting a hand on my shoulder.

Cherokee gave me a hug. "That dog is dumber than dirt sometimes, but she knows her way home."

"Y'all stay here in case she returns, okay? I'm checking the woods."

They nodded and sat on the back porch. I wanted to tell them to have one person in the front, but Sadie wasn't dumb, no matter what my niece thought. Front porch, back porch, it didn't matter. She'd know someone was outside and think it play time. She'd find them.

It was cooler among the trees. The sun broke through the thick branches of pine and autumn leaves to dapple the ground. Pine needles softened the sound of my footsteps. I called Sadie's name again, hoping for a returning bark. Nothing. I leaned against a tree. She truly was gone. There was nothing left to do but wait and pray she returned on her own.

I pulled my cell phone from my pocket and dialed Matt. "Sadie's gone. She broke free when I was at the bakery, and no one can find her anywhere."

"She'll come home, sweetheart. Why wouldn't she? You're the best thing anyone can return to."

I sniffed, encouraged by his words. "I am good to her, aren't I? When are you coming home?"

"There's no sign of Cheri. If we don't catch a break in the next day or two, I'll be back and she'll be sent to cold files. It's a shame to know who the guilty party is and not be able to locate them. I love you. Keep your chin up."

"I love you, too. I'll try." We hung up and I continued my fruitless search.

"Aunt Stormi!" Dakota's voice rang through the trees.

I turned and charged through the brush toward him. He must have found her. I burst into the backyard and skidded to a halt.

Dakota stood there, Sadie's collar in one hand and a sheet of paper in the other.

21

"What is that?" I grabbed the note.

"Some kid rode by on a skateboard and said someone paid him five dollars to bring these to us." Tears shimmered in Dakota's eyes. "Someone kidnapped Sadie."

"It'll be fine." No, it wouldn't. I reassured him out of habit as I scanned the note, reading it out loud. "Stop snooping or the dog's head is next. Instructions coming."

I would choke that woman with my bare hands when we came face-to-face. Forgive me, Lord, but I wanted to hurt her. "I need to get to the house and call Matt. You call Wayne. Tell him to come asap." I raced for the house.

I couldn't help but remember the time I had returned home to find my cats locked in the pantry. Relief flooded through me to see them still curled up on my duvet cover. What kind of sicko threatened harmless animals?

Matt didn't answer his phone, so I left a voice mail before grabbing my gun. I checked the ammo.

"What are you doing?" Dakota stood in the doorway of my office.

"Checking my gun."

"Are you going to shoot someone?"

"I might." I stuffed the Glock into the waistband of my pants as I had seen the cops do on TV. "Did you call Wayne?"

"He's on his way." Dakota peered around me. "Guns are never the answer. You said so yourself."

"Make sure you remember that." I hurriedly typed some dummy account numbers in case I ran into the dog thief, printed them off, and then pushed past him as I folded the sheet of paper and stuck it into my pocket.

"Where are you going?"

I stopped. "I have no idea." When a family member was threatened, I tended to leap before thinking.

"Hello?"

"Wayne's here." I thundered down the stairs. "Sadie's gone." I handed him the note.

"I heard." He read the note. "Did you make a copy of this? I'd like to have one."

I shook my head and handed it to Dakota who dashed back to my office. I turned back to Wayne. "What do we do now?"

"Wait for instructions. Is there any coffee?"

I exhaled sharply. "I can make some." I hated waiting.

As I measured coffee grounds, I thought over every scenario, most of them too horrible to contemplate. What if Sadie caused a problem and Cheri killed her because she was a nuisance? It could happen. Or, what if she ran away and couldn't find her way home?

"That coffee is going to be thick enough to walk on. Let me do it." Wayne dumped the grounds back into the canister and took over as my cell phone rang.

I pulled it from my pocket, thankful to see Matt's picture on my screen. "I need you."

"Why is it every time I hear those words it's because something bad has happened?"

"Sadie has been kidnapped."

"I had hoped that I had misunderstood your voice mail. I'll be home by dark."

"Thank you. I'll wait up for you."

"Tell her not to carry her gun in her waistband," Wayne yelled toward the phone. "She'll shoot off a butt cheek."

"What?" Matt asked.

"Nothing. Love you. See you later." I hung up and glared at Wayne. "Seriously? I have a license."

"That doesn't mean whoever gave it to you wasn't missing some brain cells." He pressed the button on the coffee maker.

"Ha ha." I took a seat at the table and rested my chin in my hand. My laptop! I bolted to my feet, retrieved the computer, and brought it back to the table. The instructions could very well come in an email.

I checked. Nothing.

The doorbell rang. I froze.

"I'll get it!" Dakota called out.

"No, you won't." Wayne pulled his weapon from his holster and answered the door. "It's a box." He set it on the table. "No one was there. Just this."

"Can we open it?" I peered at a box the size checks would come in.

"I will," Wayne said. "Stand back."

I moved back a few feet, my gaze glued to the box. Dakota stood next me and slipped his hand in mine.

Wayne slit the tape holding the box together and slowly lifted off the lid. "What are those?"

I moved close enough to peer inside. Little dark slivers were scattered inside. Under them was an index card that read, "I'm serious. Next time, there will be blood." I swallowed against the bile rising in my throat. "Sadie's toenail clippings."

"Better than her toes." Wayne shrugged and replaced the lid. "I'll run this to the station and check for prints. Do not leave the house. Call me if you get anything else."

I nodded and plopped back in my seat, listening for the door to close. "I can't stay here."

"Where will you go?" Dakota sat across from me. "We don't have any idea where to start looking."

"She has to be in a motel somewhere. One that allows pets." I thought of the small places dotting the highway. "I suppose she could be in a warehouse."

"That might be safer. Sadie doesn't know her and if she barked…"

"True. The warehouse seems the best place to look." I knew I wasted my breath in asking him to stay, but he shook his head before the words left my mouth. "I had to ask," I said. "Grab your jacket."

"It isn't cold."

"The warehouse is by the river. It'll be colder there." I clipped my Tazor to my pocket, slipped the cell phone inside the pocket, and grabbed a hoodie from the back of a chair. It was Cherokee's and had skull and crossbones on it, but at this point, I wasn't thinking fashion.

We left the house, I set the alarm, and we hurried to my Mercedes. "I wish we had Mom's van. It wouldn't stick out by the riverfront like this will."

"Stop by and get it," my practical nephew said.

"You know she'll want to come along." I cut him a sideways glance.

"As long as I get to ride shotgun, I don't care."

"Good boy." We sped to the bakery.

"Mom!" I burst into the shop, leaving Dakota in the car. "I need the van. I'll leave you my car."

She wiped chocolate-covered hands on a towel. "What are you up to?"

I quickly explained about Sadie's abduction and the warehouse. "I don't have time." I wiggled my fingers. "Keys, please."

"I'm coming." She untied her apron and tossed it on the counter. "Greta, man the shop." She raced past me.

"I'm driving, Mom!" No way did I want to ride in the backseat if she was driving. I tended to get carsick with her swerving.

"No time to argue, dear." She waved at Dakota to switch vehicles.

He grinned and rode shotgun, leaving me the backseat. I groaned and slammed the door shut after me. "Please, mind your driving."

"What do you mean?" Mom glanced in the rearview mirror. "I'm a careful driver. Ask anyone." She turned the key in the ignition and gunned the van into reverse. After slamming the gearshift into drive, we sped toward the highway.

Already, my stomach churned. I closed my eyes and rested my head against the window.

"Uh-oh." Mom said as the van moved to the side of the highway.

I opened my eyes and glanced behind us.

Red and blue lights flashed from the dashboard of Wayne's car. I groaned and slumped in the seat.

"I wasn't speeding," Mom said when Wayne came to the window.

"No, but I specifically told Stormi to stay home." He wore mirrored sunglasses, but I was sure he glared behind them.

"I had an idea," I said, opening one eye.

"Spare me."

"It was my idea," Dakota said.

"That's even worse. Your aunt should not involve you kids."

"I'm sixteen." Dakota crossed his arms. "I'll come along if I want. What if someone bombed the house while I was there alone?"

That thought hadn't occurred to me. "You don't think the house is in danger, do you?" I loved my old Victorian.

Wayne exhaled harshly. "Where are you going?"

We all looked at each other.

"For a drive," Mom finally said. "No law against that."

"I could take all three of you to the station for obstruction of justice."

"On what grounds?" Mom started to roll up her window, stopping only because Wayne stuck his hand in the way.

"It might take hours to determine the answer to that question."

"Move your hand."

"I will not."

She raised the window a bit more. "Your pain."

"Threatening and assaulting an officer now?"

"For crying out loud." I leaned over the seat and moved Mom's hand off the button. "You're acting like children." And it wasn't helping us find Sadie. "We'll go home."

"Promise?"

"Yes," I hissed.

"Good." He stepped back from the van.

Mom rolled up her window. "Really?"

"I didn't say *when* we would go home. Find an alternate route to the warehouse." I resumed my slump in the seat. Wayne would have to make good on his threat of arresting us to keep me from searching. I had my PI license. I could do what I wanted, right?

"I gave birth to a very devious child," Mom said, pulling back onto the highway. "Sometimes, I am rather proud of that fact."

I smiled and resumed my eyes closed, head against the window, position. I was glad Cherokee wasn't with us. She wouldn't have good memories of where we were going.

Neither did I, come to mention it. I'd almost lost her and Matt at the warehouses a month ago. I opened my eyes. "Where is Cherokee?"

"At a friend's house." Dakota glanced over his shoulder. "She has to work inventory tonight."

I relaxed. Good. At least she was accounted for and safe. Still, I checked her gps location on my phone. I'd installed the app after our last fiasco, without my families knowledge, and for my peace of mind. My niece was exactly where she said she was going to be.

My cell phone rang. It was Matt. I answered. "Hey, babe."

"Why is Wayne calling me, angry and upset because you refused to obey a direct order and are heading off with your mother and nephew to find Sadie yourselves?"

"Uh, because it's true?"

"Is that a question?"

"Yes?"

"Stop asking me questions and answer mine." He sighed. "Can't you wait for me?"

"I'll meet you at the house later. Please, understand."

"I don't, but I love you anyway. See you in a few hours." Click.

We pulled in front of the warehouses along the river. A chain link fence had been erected, sealing off the area. A large lock kept the gate securely locked against us.

I slid from the van and studied the six foot fence. If Cheri had my dog here, they had to have found a way in. "Let's circle the fence."

22

My cell phone rang…again. I was going to have to turn the volume off. "Hello?"

"Matt is almost home, and he is pissed!" Maryann's shrill voice could be heard by the others, judging from the looks on their faces. "Where are you?"

"The warehouse. Gotta go." I hung up and turned off the volume. I also had gps on my phone, so Matt could find us easily enough. One way or the other, I wasn't going home without my dog.

"Should we wait?" Mom sent a concerned look my way. "We don't want him to call off the wedding."

"Why would he do that?" He wouldn't, would he?

"Because of all the headache you cause him."

Seriously? The man loved me, faults and all. Sure, I frustrated him, but that wasn't reason enough to call off our engagement. "Let's try to find out where Sadie is being held, then we'll wait." Knowing where my baby was and not being able to snatch her back would kill me, but for the sake of love, I could control myself.

Knowing from past experience that it was best to stick together in dangerous situations, we headed around the perimeter of the shiny new fence and looked for a way in. There had to be one. Maybe Cheri could climb over if she had to, but Sadie couldn't. Unless…I handed my phone to

Dakota. "See if you can find out whether Boyd Industries owns this building."

"Yep." He handed the phone back.

Great. Cheri must have gotten a key to the padlock. I planted my fists on my hips and looked up at the curving spiked wire lining the fence. "Anyone have any gloves?"

"I am not climbing the fence." Mom shook her head. "There's a saw in the van. Cut the lock."

"Why didn't you say so before we wasted time?" I marched back to the van and stared at the empty back. "Where?"

"There are all kinds of tools under the mat. They came with the van when I bought this old thing. It must have belonged to a mechanic." Mom lifted the mat, revealing wonders of wonders, some heavy duty bolt cutters.

I grabbed them. "This is great!"

"Do you know how to use them?"

"What's there to know?" I marched up to the gate, applied the bolt cutters to the padlock, and ended up on my rearend in the gravel. "It's electrified?"

"Obviously a low voltage or you'd be dead." Mom glanced at Dakota's rubber soled shoes. "You try."

The dear boy didn't hesitate. With my heart in my throat, and my hair standing out around my head in a red halo, I watched as he stepped forward and placed the cutter against the padlock. He shook the entire gate and made a strange "uhhhh" sound.

I yanked him back.

He doubled over in laughter. "Got you. I didn't feel a thing." He dodged my fist aimed at his shoulder and cut the lock.

"Not funny at all." I took a deep breath band willed my heart rate to go back to normal. "Your mother would kill me if you died helping me." Not to mention I'd never be the same.

"Cut the shenanigans," Mom said. "We're going in."

I pulled my weapon from my waistband. "I'll be first."

Neither of them argued, although Mom did dig her own pistol from her giant purse.

I stepped through the gate and stopped to listen. No gunshots rang out, no threatening words were shouted. No dog barked.

"Maybe they aren't here," Mom said.

"They're here." Where else would they be? If not here, I was back to square one and teetering on hopelessness. *Please, God, lead me to Sadie.*

The closer we got to the warehouse, the more my apprehension grew. The last time I'd been there, the building a few doors down had had a sex-trafficking ring operating there that had almost been the end of my family. I prayed we wouldn't have to go to that particular building. Those were memories I'd rather not have to relive.

A large steel door sat open a few inches. I put my eye to the opening. Nothing but a dark corridor greeted me. Well, and a musty smell. "Sadie?" I whispered. No answering whine. We had to go in. I waved to the other two to follow me.

The door pushed open with a shrill shriek. I paused. When nothing untoward happened, I stepped into the dark and pulled by cell phone from my pocket to use the flashlight app.

"Use this instead. It has fresh batteries." Mom pulled a small flashlight from her purse.

"What all do you have in there?" I peered inside the cavernous bag. Extra ammo, a Tazor, granola bars, a bottle of water, and…what in the world? "Are those dog bones?"

"Sadie might be hungry."

I blinked back tears. "You really are the best mother in

the world."

"Thank you, dear. Now, let's keep moving." She patted my cheek. "It sure is cold in here."

I was glad I had grabbed a hoodie. The cold was damp and the sound of dripping water mingled with the increasing order of mildew led me to believe Cheri wouldn't inhabit this particular building if she could help it. I handed Dakota my cell phone again and asked him to find out which warehouses Boyd Industries owned that were close by.

"They own this entire strip," he said. "This is going to take all day."

"Sadie is worth the search." I continued down the hall, glancing into empty rooms big enough to hold semi trucks. Perhaps they once had, but this building looked as if it had been unused for a very long time.

After a fruitless search, we moved outside and to the next building. Each time we had to do that would take us closer to the nightmare from months ago. Angela, Maryann, and I had even gone as far as to try and pretend to be homeless teens so we could be adopted. No one believed our poor disguises. It wasn't until I'd gone to an abandoned motel and found Cherokee that the trouble in the warehouse really went down.

I shook off the bad memories and pushed open a peeling, red, sliding door. This one moved on well-oiled hinges. I glanced over my shoulder and held my finger to my lips. "Be ready to call the cops if anything bad happens."

Mom nodded. "Got 'em on speed dial."

They stayed so close to me, one of them stepped on the back of my Converse gym shoes. I kept going, stepping out of the shoe and into a puddle of water. There was no water dripping. Someone had recently hosed down the floors.

I shoved my foot back into my shoe and did my best to keep my gun hand steady. This was no abandoned building. Someone did business here. The question was…what kind of business and was anyone there right now? I hadn't seen any cars, but we hadn't checked the back.

"Dakota, go back to the van."

"No. I can help."

"We don't know what we're up against."

He crossed his arms. "Then we should all go back and wait for Matt."

I agreed. I thought we would find an empty building, one woman, and a dog. We might still, but we could also find much more.

Something dropped, or fell, with a thud in a room down the hall. I hesitated to check it out, but what if it was Sadie and she was injured? "Y'all stay here," I whispered. "If I need you, I'll yell."

"No, way. We stick together." Mom slid her arm through mine.

I shook her off. "I have to be able to use my arm."

"Right." She placed her hand on my shoulder.

I really hoped she didn't shoot with her gun that close to my ear.

Dakota put a hand on my other shoulder.

Together, we shuffled toward the sound I'd heard.

I plastered my back against the wall, the other two copying, and peered into the room. A cat cleaned itself from a desktop. On the floor was an empty rubber cup for holding pencils. A computer sat on the desk and on an opposite wall was a bank of hard drives. We'd found the heart of something…maybe Boyd Industries. Suddenly, I wanted to be anywhere but where we were.

I straightened. "I don't think Sadie is here. She would have smelled me and barked."

"Unless she's muzzled," Dakota pointed out.

Great. We had to keep going.

We came to a T-junction. Right or left? I closed my eyes

and waited for guidance, really wishing I'd waited for Matt or Wayne. I chose left.

Somewhere down the hall, footsteps scraped. We froze. The footsteps stopped. Someone was following us and didn't want us to know they were there. I pushed open a door and shoved Dakota inside. "Stay there and lock this door."

"No. It looks like a prison cell."

It did, holding nothing more than a cot and a small end table. The bed was made and an empty beer bottle was on the floor. Someone spent time in there recently.

"You listen to me, young man." Mom stepped forward. "You stay put like—"

I pushed her inside and locked the door from my side. "I'm sorry." I raced away, hoping they'd have the sense to stay out of sight. The moment Mom wanted to come along, I should have ditched her and Dakota. But, I'd seriously thought we'd find Sadie in a cage, I'd punch Cheri in the face, and we'd be gone before she picked herself up off the ground. Sometimes, I was an optimistic idiot.

The footsteps came closer and faster. I needed to find a place of my own, and fast.

I turned another corner and came to a dead end. A room branched off of each side of the hall. The door on my right was locked. I charged through the one on my left, slapped the automatic light off, and squatted in the corner, my gun at the ready.

My heart pounded in my ears, drowning out all sound. I was blind and deaf with someone chasing me, and I was cornered. I'd have to shoot my way to freedom. *Please, God, don't let me die.*

My pursuer stopped in the doorway. It was a big, hulking man, his face in shadows. He carried a hand gun.

What was he waiting for? Maybe he would move on and I wouldn't have to shoot. Oh, please, please, please...no such luck. He stepped inside.

I kept as still as possible. Maybe he didn't know I was in there? No, he had to know. There was nowhere else. Yes, I could have gone into the locked room. I could have been the one to lock the door. Was it possible if I made no sound he would think that very thing?

No. He took another step inside. "I know you're in here. Come on out."

I closed my eyes and pulled the trigger.

"What the hell, Stormi?" Wayne dove to the side.

"What are you doing here?" I rushed to turn on the light.

"Trying to find you and provide backup to a woman with no sense." He got to his feet. "Matt said to tell you to wait. He'll be here in an hour."

"Did you see the computers?"

"Yeah. Good find."

A scream came from down the hall.

23

Wayne and I rushed to the room where I had locked Mom and Dakota. I pressed my face against the window in the door. "What's wrong?"

"I heard a gunshot. I thought someone had killed you." Mom rattled the door handle. "Let us out."

I flipped the lock. "I almost killed Wayne, but it's all good now."

"Speak for yourself." He glared and shook his head. "Dakota, without argument, I want you to take your cell phone and—"

"I don't have a cell phone."

"Why doesn't this young man have a phone?" Wayne glanced at me.

"I'm not his mother, and she refuses to spend the money."

"You have plenty of money. Get him a phone." He dug a phone out of his pocket. "Take this to the van and lock yourself in. No arguing. I need eyes out there. You call me if you see anything at all. We don't want to be caught by surprise." He put a hand on Dakota's shoulder. "Can you do this?"

Eyes wide, Dakota nodded.

"Good. Now, be careful not to be seen and go straight there. Text your aunt when you're locked in."

Dakota took off like a flash.

"I wish I had somewhere to send you, Anne, but I don't. Stick close to me." Wayne exhaled sharply. "I give up on Stormi."

"Gee, thanks."

Mom showed him her gun. "I'm ready for whatever comes."

"Lord, spare me from the Nelson women. I'm dating the only sane one."

That was debatable. "What now?"

"I don't think your dog or her abductor are here. We check the next building."

The one I dreaded stepping foot inside of. I took a deep breath. I could do this.

Staying to the deepening shadows, we skirted the building and headed for the largest warehouse in the line. I knew the secrets the walls held, the rooms underground, the evil soaked into the bricks and mortar. My skin crawled the closer we got, and my steps lagged.

"Come on," Mom whispered. "Do you want to be left behind?"

I shook my head, almost saying yes. Wayne could handle things from here. Matt would arrive soon. There was no need for me to go into that place. I grabbed Mom's arm. "Let Wayne handle it."

"Alone?" She frowned. "I thought you wanted to rescue your dog?"

"Yeah, but that building…"

"It's okay. Those things aren't happening in there anymore. It's just an empty warehouse."

"Right."

She patted my cheek. "You'll be fine. We have God on our side."

"Yes." I squared my shoulders. "I'm ready now."

"That's my girl."

Wayne had waited for us at the corner, ready to dart across the open space between the buildings. To me, it looked the size of a football field, but was more like fifty feet. If anyone was watching, they'd spot us for sure and we would lose the element of surprise.

My phone vibrated in my pocket. It was a text from Dakota letting us know he was in the van and hunkered down in the front seat. Good. If we needed to make a fast getaway, he could drive up and get us.

Wayne started making sign gestures with his hands.

"I have no idea what you're trying to say," I said. Maybe I should learn cop sign language, but I didn't have time then.

"Good grief. We'll go across one at a time. Don't go until I wave you across. Be as silent and as fast as possible."

My heart beat in my throat, the sound of it loud enough to drown out all other sound, if there were any. Instead, a pall of heavy silence hung over the property. I kept my eyes glued on Wayne's back, wishing with all in me that Matt was standing by my side. No one's fault but my own. If I'd waited, he would be next to me.

Wayne reached the shadow of the other building in seconds. The sun had gone completely down, leaving us only star light to see by. A full moon would have been nice.

"Go, Mom."

"You first."

I shook my head. "I'll bring up the rear. Go!"

She raced away, fast for a fifty-year-old woman. Fear did that to you, set wings to your feet.

All too soon it was my turn. I took several deep breaths and ran, my legs bumping. I passed Wayne and plastered my back to the cool cement wall. "I made it. That wasn't so bad."

"Stay close." Wayne led us to a back door. The door

squeaked as it opened. The same door that led to the same hallway I'd pretended to be a runaway teen and lived in for a night. The same hall that held the room where Cherokee had been drugged and held prisoner. The same hall in which I witnessed Matt's beating.

I stood in the doorway and listened. No sounds alerted me to anyone's presence. No cries of abducted girls or gleeful taunts from perverted men reached my ears. Some of my tension resided. Mom was right. It was nothing more than a building.

Our footsteps echoed in the empty space. Wayne, glancing in each room we passed, stayed in front, leading us in a fearless march onward. What was it about him and Matt that gave them the courage to head into dangerous situations? With Mom, it was sense of adventure, me a drive for justice, both misguided most of the time.

Wayne held up his hand. "It's the main room. There is a single light bulb hanging from the ceiling. We can see, but visibility is limited. Same procedure as outside. Try not to stomp your feet."

Mom gripped my hand. "There's no party to cater this time."

No, things could get very real. If Cheri had Sadie within these walls, she'd already proven she had no qualms about killing. We could be picked off as we crossed that room.

Wayne didn't run this time, instead he seemed to pick his steps, moving like a ghost across the dust-covered floor. Mom copied him, waving at me when she reached the other side.

This was it. I took a step into the room.

A shot rang out from above us, kicking up dirt and chipping the floor at my feet. "Welcome to my humble abode. Drop your weapon and kick it away from you."

"Cheri, I want my dog." I didn't move.

"I want those account numbers. Let's make a trade. Now, drop the gun and your friends will live."

I dropped the gun and kicked it two feet away, then pulled the papers from my pocket and waved them in the air. "Come and get them." I hadn't been aware the building had an upper floor that looked down to where I stood.

"So that brute of a cop can take me down? I don't think so. Leave them there and go back the way you came. I'll release the dog. She'll find you."

Wayne motioned for me to keep her talking, then slipped into the opposite hallway.

"You don't get anything until I see for myself that Sadie is unharmed."

"You really aren't in any condition to make demands, Stormi. I could shoot you where you stand, take out the other two, kill your dog, and take the papers."

"You could." I glanced at Mom. "Do you have a lighter in that bag of yours?"

"Of course, I do." She dug it out and tossed it to me.

Miracle of miracles, I caught it in my left hand. I ignited it and held it a few inches from the paper in my hand. "You could shoot me, but I'll set these on fire and you'll be back to square one."

She cursed. The sound of pounding feet told me she'd gone.

I almost sagged with relief. I thought for sure she'd call my bluff and leave me lying in a puddle of my own blood.

Wayne yelled from somewhere within the recesses of the building. A door slammed, then pounding.

Mom raced to my side, grabbed my arm, and yanked me into the hallway we'd left. We huddled together, waiting for some sign Wayne was all right. From the yells and curses echoing through the building, we knew he wasn't dead.

"Did she trap him?" Mom's mouth fell open. She

snapped it shut. "How does anyone get the drop on that man?"

"I don't know. Let's head outside and wait for Matt." At least we knew Sadie was close. My cell phone alerted me to a text.

Matt is in the building.

Good boy, Dakota. I slipped the phone back into my pocket. Where are you, Matt? I headed for the end of the hall and glanced out into the night, before pulling the door closed except for a couple of inches. If someone came in that way, we'd know.

"We have to find Matt," I said.

Mom nodded. "How many ways are there into this building?"

"That's the only one I know of." I wanted to call for him, but that would only alert Cheri to his presence.

"Stormi!" Speak of the devil. Her voice came from the room we'd just left. "Step out where I can see you."

"I don't think so."

"Do it or that big cop dies."

Drat. After all Wayne had done for me, I couldn't let that happen. "Mom, you stay here. Run for help if you have to."

"I think it's time for help, dear. I'm calling the police."

"Matt and Wayne are here. There are only a couple of officers left and Maryann will kill me if something happens to her boyfriend. Leave him safe at the precinct. If Matt wants backup, he'll call."

"Don't make me say it again." Cheri's voice rose, shrill with stress.

"I love you Mom." I gave her a quick hug, shoved the papers into her hands, and stepped into the open.

"Give me the papers." Cheri pointed a handgun at my chest.

Purchasing a Kevlar vest was going to be at the top of my

next-to-buy list…if I lived through this. "Hidden. If you shoot me, you'll never get them. You'll have to skip the country."

"I don't have the money to skip the country, you idiot. Why do you think I'm doing this?"

I crossed my arms. "If you want me to feel sorry for you, it isn't going to work."

"Shut up and let me think."

"What did you do with Wayne?"

"Shut up!" She fired a shot over my head, raining plaster on us like gray snow.

Mom peeked around the corner.

"Get over here." Cheri waved her over with the gun. "Leave your purse on that crate. Now, the two of you sit down, backs agains that wall." She motioned toward the wall closest to us but away from either hall entrance. She kicked my gun a few more feet away from where I sat, then perched on a crate and stared at us.

"What?" I narrowed my eyes.

She didn't say anything, just kept her gaze glued on us. I guess she needed to do some heavy duty thinking.

Mom started to say something, but clamped her lips together when I elbowed her. Cheri had come unhinged more than she had been. I wasn't going to provoke her unless I found a way out of the mess we were in.

"I wish I had something to tie you up with." Cheri got up and riffled through Mom's purse. "What? No zip ties or duct tape? You have everything else." She opened a granola bar and resumed her seat. "Except my papers. Now, I wonder where you could have hidden them."

I shrugged. Mom could have stuck them anywear.

"I could strip search you, I suppose, but that sounds a bit gross, even to me." Cheri wadded up the wrapper to the granola bar and tossed it on the floor. "You two want a bone?" She laughed and called us the B-word that rhymed with witch.

She had that wrong in my opinion. The title fit her much better. Since her silence had made me uncomfortable, I decided to give her the same treatment.

A noise sounded from the hall.

Cheri whirled as Matt stepped into sight.

She pulled the trigger.

He fell.

I screamed.

24

Cheri removed Matt's weapon and tossed it on top of a box.

"Matt!" I pushed her out of the way and rushed to his side, falling to my knees.

He opened one eye. "Go away," he said, under his breath. "Vest."

"Come over here, Stormi," Cheri ordered. "No man is ever worth a woman's tears. You would do well to remember that."

"This man is." I didn't have to fake tears as I planted a kiss on his lips. I stood and shuffled next to Mom, who sobbed into her hands. I wanted to tell her Matt lived, but didn't want her to let slip anything that would alert Cheri who had taken to staring at us again.

Matt slid an inch toward the door, making a rasping sound.

Cheri didn't budge. "Isn't this the point in every story where you ask me why?"

"I know why. There are millions of dollars in those off shore accounts."

"Which you will never get!" Mom spit. "I burned them."

Cheri's gun hand swung toward Mom. "Then there is no reason to keep you around, is there?"

Mom's eyes widened. "I didn't really."

"Of course, you didn't. I can see that you aren't a fool. You need some leverage to hold over my head, just as the dog is my leverage over you. Well, the dog and that cop I locked into the room he ducked into when I shot at him."

I exhaled long and deep. Wayne wasn't injured.

Matt moved his fingers in a talking motion.

"So, since you seem to be in a talking mood, why kill Seth? What part did he play in the illegal finances of Boyd? Didn't he quit because he wanted no part of it?"

She blinked rapidly. "His death was an unfortunate accident." Tears welled in her eyes. "I loved him, you see. We met at a Boyd Industries function and hooked up. He wouldn't leave his wife for me, so I decided to eliminate the opposition. I had no idea the man enjoyed bubble baths."

"Surely you knew he and Shelby had a thing going on for quite a while." I watched Matt move another inch. How long did he expect me to talk?

She looked shocked. "I can't kill family."

"So, realizing your mistake, you killed Amber."

She waved the gun. "Don't forget my cleaning up loose ends. I thought the wounded bear was a nice touch."

"Was it me you wanted to get rid of, or any of my party in general?" Matt was directly behind her now and getting to his feet.

Mom's eyes widened. "Oh."

Exactly why I didn't say anything.

Cheri turned as Matt lunged for her. Her gun went off again, knocking him back.

I pounced on her back like a spider monkey, wrapping my legs around her waist and hanging on with all I had.

Mom scrambled on the floor after my gun. "Hold her still, Stormi!"

"I'm trying."

Cheri held the gun over her head and pointed at me as

Matt moved toward her again. "She's too close for me to miss, cop. Don't take another step."

He held up his hands.

"Down on your knees, handsome. Mrs. Nelson, you join him. Stormi, if you don't get off me, they both die."

I slid from her back and joined my loved ones. We knelt on the floor, hands folded behind our heads and stared up at her.

"Now, this is a mess." She sighed. "What to do, what to do." She paced, keeping the pistol aimed at us. After several minutes, she smiled and stopped in front of Matt. She caressed his face with the barrel of the gun. "You sure are pretty. Too bad I didn't meet your before…all this." She straightened. "Not that I like most men. I haven't had good luck with them, but you seem like one of the good ones. How about running away with me? I'm going to be a very wealthy woman."

"No, thanks. I'll keep the woman I've got, thank you." A muscle ticked in his jaw.

"Your loss." She perched back on the crate. "I've tried to think of everything possible not to have you kill you three. I've lost my stomach for killing, not that I enjoyed it much to begin with. But, I cannot see a way out of this."

"I do." Lawrence Boyd stepped into the room, a revolver trained on Cheri. "You didn't think I would find out, did you? Little sneak, after the money I worked so hard for. Tsk tsk."

She laughed. "Now, this is an interesting turn of events. You're a bit old for my taste, but how about we knock these three off and head to Europe together."

"So you can kill me? No, thanks. I've had enough of you and your cousin. I've already got my flight booked and won't be around long enough to form an attachment to anyone new."

Cheri hopped off her crate and the two circled each other like jungle cats. "I don't aim to let that money go. I've debts to pay."

"Not my problem."

I let my hands down in a vain effort to still the sharp ache in my shoulders. As those two warred with words, I glanced around for my gun. There.

I scrambled on hands and knees. I grabbed it and tossed it to Matt.

He caught it and fired, knocking Mom to the ground. His first shot took Cheri in the leg, the second one took Boyd in the side. They both fell.

I retrieved Mom's gun from her purse, while she disarmed the two injured ones. With four guns trained on them, they weren't going anywhere.

"Good job, sweetheart," Matt grinned, giving me a one-armed hug. "We make a good team."

"The best." My cell phone vibrated. It was a text from Dakota informing me he'd called the police because of all the gunfire and hoped I was alive to read the text. I answered back that I was fine. "Calvary is on its way."

"I can handle things here," Matt said. "Go free Wayne and find Sadie."

"Thank you." I darted into the opposite hall.

"Let me out." Wayne stuck his arms through bars in a door window. "What's going on out there?"

I slid the bolt to free him. "Everything is under control. Matt and Mom are holding the killers at gunpoint in the main room."

"I'll see what I can do." He rushed away.

I'd kind of hoped he would help me look for my dog. "Sadie!"

A scratching sounded to my right. I hurried further down a dark hall. "Where are you, girl?"

She whined behind a wooden door. I flung it open and fell to my knees as my muzzled baby launched herself at me. The force of her body slamming into mine threw me against the wall. My head struck concrete and everything went black.

When I woke, I was lying in the back of an ambulance, Sadie leaning on the bumper and looking inside, while Matt held my hand. "I survive having a gun pointed at me only to have my dog knock me out."

He chuckled, rubbing his thumb across the back of my hand. "Life is never boring with you, Stormi." He leaned over and pressed his lips against mine.

At that point, I wasn't sure whether my dizziness was from the knock to the head or his kiss. I do know I felt an emptiness when he pulled away. "A Christmas wedding?"

He shook his head. "I was hoping for Spring. I know it's further away, but I've seen pictures of the strapless wedding gown you cut out of a magazine and *really* want to see you in it."

Anything for my prince. "You aren't supposed to be snooping. Okay, spring it is. Now, kiss me again."

He obliged, until someone cleared their throat. "Hold off on that for a while," Wayne said. "We've got to stop Shelby at the airport. Lawrence said she has the account numbers and is skipping town. It seems our little bride wasn't as innocent as she tried to be."

"I'm coming." I sat up, my head spinning.

"Oh, no, you don't."

"Matt! I have to see this through." I got up, keeping my hand on the wall of the ambulance until things stopped spinning. "I can wait in the car, but I am coming."

"Fine." He jumped to the ground and held out his hand.

We sped away in a squad car to the airport just under an hour away. Wayne seemed to know where he was going, so Matt and I followed him onto the runway where Boyd's private jet waited.

In the hangar, Shelby perched on a stool, a cup of tea in one hand, her shapely legs crossed. She saw us and sighed. "Darn. Can't a girl do anything without someone stopping her?"

"Not if it's illegal." Wayne pulled his handcuffs.

"Don't use those. I'm coming. I guess dear old Lawrence ratted on me. That's fine. Daddy will bail me out." She sashayed to the car and slid into the back seat.

Of course, I hadn't stayed in the car as promised and slid in after her. "I guess you needed money after your engagement broke up."

She shrugged. "Can you blame me? Daddy has money, but he refuses to give me any." She pouted. "I'm sure he will now. He won't want his name tarnished with me serving jail time."

"Who is your father, Shelby?"

She gave a sly grin. "Stepdaddy, actually. Milton Boyd, Lawrence's brother."

I wanted to throw up. I scooted away from her so her dirty lifestyle didn't brush off on me. Thank goodness God kept me on the straight and narrow. Being a best-selling author could easily go to my head and I could live a dirty lifestyle. I chose not to. I stared at the back of Matt's head and thanked God for such a good man.

I closed my eyes and rested my head against the back of the plastic seat. When I opened them, we were pulling in front of the police station and Matt was opening the door for me.

"Come on gorgeous." He held out his hand.

Shelby's eyes widened. "I guess it really is true. Beauty is in the eyes of the beholder. He thinks you pretty in stained jeans and ripped tee shirt, no makeup, and mussed hair."

I grinned. "That's the beauty of bringing the bad to

justice." I waved my arm in a courtly bow. "Have a good life." I linked my arm in Matt's and did my best sashay imitation of Shelby into the building.

"If the Justice of the Peace were here," Matt said, his eyes stormy, "I'd marry you right now, dirt and all."

"I might even let you." I kissed him. "Go book that gal and take me home."

"Gladly." He took Shelby's arm and escorted her out of sight.

Our little precinct was quiet that time of the night. I spread out on the chairs and closed my eyes again. It had been a long glorious day. I fell asleep dreaming of my father and how happy he must be to know the Grangers received their justice.

The End

ABOUT THE AUTHOR

Website at www.cynthiahickey.com

Multi-published and Amazon and ECPA Best-Selling author Cynthia Hickey has sold close to a million copies of her works since 2013. She has taught a Continuing Education class at the 2015 American Christian Fiction Writers conference, several small ACFW chapters and RWA chapters, and small writer retreats. She and her husband run the small press, Winged Publications, which includes some of the CBA's best well-known authors. She lives in Arizona and Arkansas, becoming a snowbird, with her husband and one dog. She has ten grandchildren who keep her busy and tell everyone they know that "Nana is a writer".

Connect with me on FaceBook
Twitter
Bookbub
Sign up for my newsletter and receive a free short story
www.cynthiahickey.com

Follow me on Amazon

Enjoy other mysteries by Cynthia Hickey

Nosy Neighbor Series
<u>Anything For A Mystery</u>, **Book 1**
<u>A Killer Plot</u>, **Book 2**
<u>Skin Care Can Be Murder</u>, **Book 3**

www.ingramcontent.com/pod-product-compliance
Lightning Source LLC
Chambersburg PA
CBHW070306120726
47910CB00007B/2381